HISTORY OF ISLAM

A Reader Series

Suitable for grade six (Age group 10+)

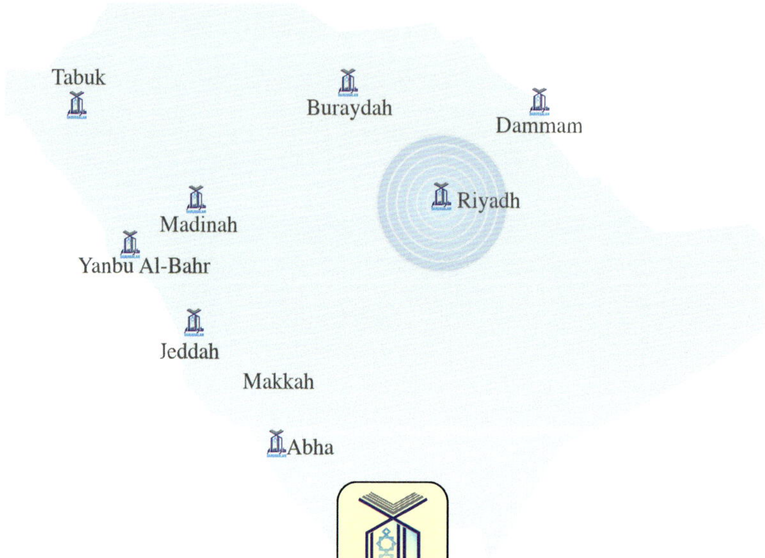

DARUSSALAM

YOUR AUTHENTIC SOURCE OF KNOWLEDGE

HEAD OFFICE

Prince Abdul Aziz
Bin Jalawi street.
P.O.Box: 22743,
Riyadh 11416
K.S.A.
Tel: 00966 -1- 4033962
00966 -1- 4043432
Fax: 00966 -1- 4021659
E-mail:
info@darussalam.com
darussalam@awalnet.net.sa
Website:
www.darussalamksa.com

K.S.A. Darussalam Showrooms:

- **Riyadh**
  Olaya branch:
  Tel: 00966-1-4614483
  Fax: 4644945
  Malaz branch:
  Tel: 00966-1-4735220
  Fax: 4735221
  Suwaydi branch:
  Tel 00966-1-4286641
  Suwailam branch:
  Tel & Fax:
  00966-1-2860422
- **Jeddah**
  Tel: 00966-2-6879254
  Fax: 6336270
- **Madinah**
  Tel: 00966-04-8234446,
  8230038 Fax: 04-8151121
- **Al-Khobar**
  Tel: 00966-3-8692900
  Fax:00966-3-8691551
- **Khamis Mushayt**
  Tel & Fax: 00966-072207055
- **Yanbu Al-Bahr**
  Tel: 0500887341
  Fax: 8691551
- **Al-Buraida**
  Tel: 0503417156
  Fax: 00966-06-3696124

The Age of the Rightly-Guided Caliphs:

AL- Khulafa ar-Rashidùn

Umar ibn al-Khattab

The Second of the Four Rightly-Guided Caliphs

Maulvi Abdul Aziz

MA; D. Ed [London]

DARUSSALAM

YOUR AUTHENTIC SOURCE OF KNOWLEDGE

Riyadh • Jeddah • Al-Khobar • Sharjah

Lahore • London • Houston • New York

بسم الله الرحمن الرحيم

In the Name of Allah,
the Most Gracious, the Most Merciful

King Fahd National Library Cataloging-in-Publication Data

Abdul Aziz, Moulavi

Umar Ibn-Khattab. / Moulavi Abdul Aziz .- Riyadh 2012

142 p : 17cm X 24 cm

ISBN: 978-603-500-077-2

1-Prophet Companion Successers 2- Omar ibn ,
Al-Khattab ibn Naufal , 23 H.- Biography 3-Caliphs
I.Title

239.9 dc 1433/1217

L.D. no. 1433 / 1217
ISBN: 978-603-500-077-2

Publisher's Note

In the Name of Allah, the Lord of Grace, the Ever Merciful

For many years, I have been looking for textbooks on the History of Islam for English-speaking students, yet I have found very few. Most did not overcome a common problem: they did not go beyond the era of the Four Rightly-Guided Caliphs, may Allah be pleased with them all.

Bearing this in mind, we, at Darussalam, have resolved to present the entire History of Islam to our youth in language that appeals to them, in a simple yet lucid manner. The first four volumes in this series explore Islamic history during the period of the first Four Rightly-Guided Caliphs. Later volumes would be devoted to the History of Islam, down through the ages to modern times, in sha' Allah.

Our past, present, and future are interconnected and interdependent. Therefore, knowing and understanding our history is not optional; it is essential.

This is the second volume from this series, which deals with the life of Umar ibn al-Khattab, the second of the Four Rightly-Guided Caliphs. The evaluation of Umar, may Allah be pleased with him, and his far-sighted policies is captured in a statement attributed to the Prophet, 'There were in the nations before you "inspired people", and if there is any one of them in my nation, it is Umar.'

We would like to thank the author Maulvi Abdul Aziz, the editor and the designer Mr. Shahzad Ahmed for their diligent efforts in preparing this volume. We hope this work will inspire our youth to form a personal relationship with Umar ibn al-Khattab and encourage them to commit their lives sincerely to the mission of 'Al-Faruq', that is, discerning truth from falsehood, which he has left behind as our common heritage.

Abdul Malik Mujahid

Muharram 23, 1433

Darussalam, Riyadh

December 18, 2011

Chapter 1

Chapter 2

Chapter 3

Chapter 4

Chapter 5

Chapter 6

Chapter 7

Contents

Umar ibn al-Khattab

The Second of the Four Rightly-Guided Caliphs

Umar ibn al-Khattab

The Second of the Four Rightly-Guided Caliphs

After the death of Abu Bakr as-Siddiq ﷺ, Umar ibn al-Khattab ﷺ became the leader of the Muslim nation or *Ummah*. The Muslims took *Bai'ah* or the oath of loyalty at the hand of Umar, in Madinah on Tuesday, 23 Jumada al-Akhirah, in the year 13 AH/634 CE. Before his death, Abu Bakr had named Umar as his successor – a decision that apparently met with no resistance from the large community. There was good reason for this general acceptance. Umar enjoyed a very high status due to his record of early and enormous service to Islam.

Umar succeeded Abu Bakr whose official title was *Khalifat Rasul Allah* or the Successor to the Messenger of Allah ﷺ. Thus, Umar was first called *Khalifat Khalifat Rasul Allah,* meaning Successor to the Successor of the Messenger of Allah. People realized that repetition of the word *Khalifah* would prove awkward to use in daily speech. Thus, he adopted the title *Amir al-Mu'minîn*: Commander or Leader of the Believers. This sounded more attractive to the Muslims, since it was shorter, easier and more suitable for common use. *Amir al-Mu'minîn* henceforth became the title of the lawful ruler of the nation after him. The Arabic term *Amir* stresses the role of the leader primarily as a counsellor or guide, which is quite fitting for the Caliph's position. Some scholars have appropriately translated the title *Amir al-Mu'minîn* as 'First Counsellor'. The Caliphate of Umar marked the period when one of the most outstanding political leaders – not only of Islam but in the history of the world – took over the command of state affairs at Madinah.

> "Umar adopted the title of Amir *al-Mu'minîn* It was shorter, easier and more suitable for common use."

When the *Bai'ah* or declaration

of loyalty or allegiance by the people was over, Umar ascended the pulpit and addressed the people assembled in the Mosque:

> 'Abu Bakr is no more with us. He successfully ran the affairs of the *Ummah* for more than two years. I wish the responsibility of leading the nation had fallen on someone else. I never desired such a position. I do not want to put myself on the same level as Abu Bakr.'

After this, he went down one step, praised Allah, and then said:

> 'I promise that I shall not run away from this responsibility. I shall fulfil my duty to the best of my ability. I shall seek guidance from the Qur'an, from the teachings of the Messenger of Allah ﷺ and the example set by Abu Bakr in running the affairs of the State. In this work, I will also seek your participation and help. If I am right, follow me; if I deviate, correct me so that we may not go astray. Many of you say that I was harsh during the lifetime of the Messenger of Allah ﷺ, and uncompromising during Abu Bakr's rule. Yes, whenever they sought my opinion, I gave my opinion. Sometimes they accepted my opinion, and sometimes they rejected it. However, thanks to Allah, the Messenger of Allah ﷺ was pleased with me, and so was Abu Bakr. Now that the responsibility has fallen on me, I shall try to be gentle and tender. However, I shall be stern and strict against an aggressor in favour of the weak and poor.'

Umar then sought Allah's blessings and the people's co-operation in running the affairs of the state.

The Early Life
of Umar ibn al-Khattab

Umar ibn al-Khattab was born in a clan of the Quraysh in Makkah, thirteen years after the Year of the Elephant. He was white with a reddish complexion. He had handsome cheeks, nose, eyes and large hands and feet. He was muscular, tall and bald. He was very strong and bold. When he walked, he walked quickly; when he spoke, he spoke clearly, and when he struck, he caused pain.

His father was al-Khattab ibn Nufayl. His mother was Hantamah bint Hashim, the sister of Abu Jahl. He had thirteen children in all: nine sons and four daughters. One of his daughters, Hafsah, was married to the Messenger of Allah ﷺ after his migration to Madinah. The total number of his wives was seven - including those whom he married during the time of Ignorance (*Jahiliyyah*) and Islam, as well as those he divorced, who died or were left behind after his death.

He was one of the few Makkans who were able to read and write. He bore responsibility at an early age. He had a very harsh upbringing devoid of wealth and luxury. His father al-Khattab forced him to tend his camels. His father's harsh treatment had a negative effect on Umar, which he remembered all his life. This was a period of hardship during Umar's life.

> "Umar was one of the few Makkans who were able to read and write."

Once, when Umar went for *Hajj* and reached Dajnan (a mountain situated at a distance of some 25 kilometres from Makkah), he said, 'There is no God but Allah, the Most High, the Most Great, the One Who gives whatever He Wills to whomever He wills! I used to tend the camels of al-Khattab in this valley, wearing a woollen garment. He was harsh. He would exhaust me when I worked and beat me if I fell short. And now here I am, with no one between me and Allah!'

Umar did not just tend livestock for his father, he used to tend the animals of his maternal aunts as well. In return for it, they would give him a handful of dates or raisins, which would suffice him for the day. Tending livestock made Umar acquire good qualities such as patience, toughness, and self-control. Umar was also a famous sportsman from his early youth and excelled in all kinds of sports, such as wrestling, riding and horsemanship.

He earned a reputation as a wrestler. He enjoyed and narrated poetry. He was interested in history and the current affairs of his people. By profession, he was a trader. He would engage in trade and learn the history of the Arabs and the battles and conflicts that had occurred among the tribes. Trade made Umar one of the rich men of Makkah. He was introduced to many people in the lands that he visited for the purpose of trade and became familiar with their customs. He travelled to Syria in the summer and Yemen in winter.

People used to come to him to settle their disputes and he would judge between the Arabs regarding their disputes before Islam. Umar resisted Islam in the

Ruins of Okaz Market

beginning, because he feared that this new Faith would shake the system that was well-established in Makkah. Makkah enjoyed a special status among the Arabs. It was the site of the Sacred House to which people came for pilgrimage. This gave the Quraysh a unique status among the Arabs. It brought material wealth to Makkah. This was the reason for the city's prosperity and its people's enormous wealth. Thus, the rich men of Makkah stood up against Islam. They tortured the weak among those who accepted Islam, and Umar too was at the forefront of those who persecuted the weak Muslims. Even so, because of his outstanding qualities and bravery, Umar enjoyed enormous power and influence in Arabia.

Umar's Acceptance of Islam

Umar's heart was moved on the day when he saw some women of the Quraysh leaving Makkah and travelling to Ethiopia, a distant land, because of the persecution that they were facing from him and others like him. His conscience was stirred. He felt remorse and pity for them. He spoke kind words to them, which they had never expected to hear from someone like Umar. He wondered: what was the secret behind this extraordinary strength? He felt sad and his heart was filled with pain.

Shortly afterwards, Umar embraced Islam. The main reason behind his acceptance of Islam was the *Du'â* or supplication of the Messenger of Allah ﷺ as we shall learn shortly.

Umar's Decision to Kill the Messenger of Allah ﷺ

Once, the Quraysh met to discuss the matter of the Prophet ﷺ. They asked each other, 'Who will kill him?' Umar responded, 'I will do it.' Umar had been one of the most unbending enemies of the Prophet of Allah ﷺ and his mission. He was devoted to the pagan cult centred on the Ka'bah and used to blame the Prophet ﷺ for dividing the loyalties of the Quraysh by questioning their ancient pagan religion.

As he left his home in fury with his sword in hand, he met a friend who had become a Muslim but he had not made public his Islam for fear of the Quraysh. 'Where are you heading, O Umar?' asked his friend Nu'aym ibn Abdullah. Umar said, 'I am looking for the one who has changed his religion, who has divided the Quraysh, criticized their religion and slandered their gods. I am going to kill him.' Nu'aym at once responded, 'Have you any idea what will happen if you kill him?' The entire tribe of Banu Abd Manâf will take their revenge on you.'

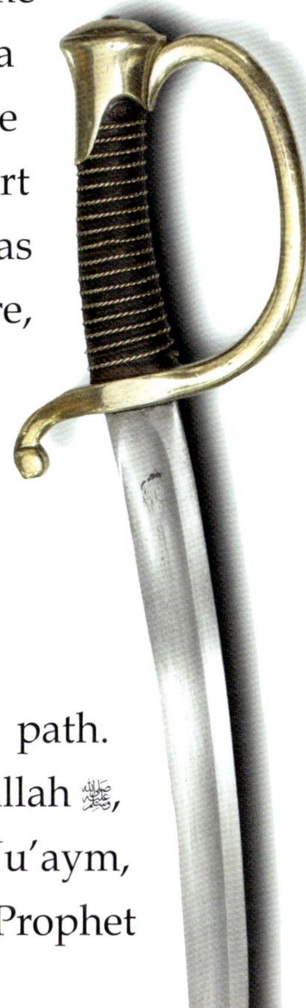

They argued until their voices became loud. 'It seems you too have become a Muslim,' Umar remarked furiously. He added, 'If I find it to be true, I shall start with you.' Nu'aym realized that it was not possible to stop Umar. He, therefore, revealed, 'Let me tell you that your sister Fatimah and her husband have accepted Islam. They have abandoned you and the misguidance that you follow.'

Suddenly, Umar changed his path. Instead of going to the Messenger of Allah ﷺ, he headed toward his sister's home. Nu'aym, obviously, went straight to inform the Prophet of Allah ﷺ.

Umar loved his sister very much, but his fury and hatred against Islam made him lose all sense. When the furious Umar reached their home, Fatimah and her husband were reciting a *Sûrah* of the Qur'an written on a parchment, under the instruction of another Muslim named Khabbab. On hearing his irate voice at the door, Khabbab hid from Umar. Fatimah immediately hid the parchment as soon as she noticed Umar entering her home. Nevertheless, Umar had already seen it. When he questioned them, both Fatimah and her husband confessed that they had accepted Islam. They had concealed it for fear of the Quraysh. Upon hearing this, Umar struck his brother-in-law. When his sister sprang up to defend him, he struck her as well and drew blood. However, at the sight of his wounded sister he was overcome with regret. Seeing his changed expression, Fatimah said, 'O enemy of Allah! Are you hitting me, because I believe in Allah alone?' He said, 'Yes.' She said, 'Do what you like. I bear witness that there is no god except Allah and that Muhammad is the Messenger of Allah. We have become Muslims whether you like it or not.'

When Umar heard this, he regretted what he had done. He realized that he had behaved in a senseless manner. When he calmed down, Umar asked Fatimah and her husband to show him what they were reciting before his arrival. However, Fatimah told him he could not touch it, because he was not clean.

So Umar washed himself and then took the parchment of the Qur'an to see what his sister and brother-in-law were reading. Umar saw *Sûrah Ta Hâ* and some other *Sûrahs* (chapters of the Qur'an) were written on it. He saw on it the words: *'Bismillâh ir-Rahmânir Rahîm'* [In the Name of Allah, the Most Gracious the Most Merciful]. When he read the words *ar-Rahmân* and *ar-Rahîm*, he was amazed. He began to read *Sûrah TaHâ* [*Sûrah* 20: 1-8] and felt a growing respect and awe for the words. He said, 'How beautiful and noble are these words!' When Khabbab heard this, he came out from his hiding-place and said, 'Umar, I have hope that Allah has chosen you through the supplication of His Prophet whom I heard praying yesterday, "O Allah! Strengthen Islam with Abu'l Hakam, the son of Hisham, or with Umar, the son of al-Khattab!" 'O Khabbab,' said Umar, 'Where will Allah's Messenger be now, that I may go to him and enter Islam?' Tears of joy flowed from the eyes of Fatimah and her husband. It was the happiest moment for them.

Umar then went to the Prophet ﷺ and declared his

intention to become a Muslim. '*Allahu Akbar!* [Allah is Great]' exclaimed the Prophet ﷺ, in such a way that every man and woman there came to know that Umar had entered Islam, and they all rejoiced.

Umar's conversion was a turning point in the fortunes of the Muslim community. The addition of his strong personality greatly increased the prestige of the small community of Muslims. Umar's acceptance of Islam was a means of greater power; his migration to Madinah brought about victory and his caliphate was an act of Allah's mercy. The Prophet ﷺ himself once supplicated to Allah for help by Umar's conversion. The Prophet's ﷺ supplication was answered, and a day later, in Dhul Hijjah, in the sixth year of Prophethood, Umar embraced Islam. He was then twenty-seven years old. From that day onward, the influence of the Muslim community continued to grow until it reached its summit in the majestic empire created by Umar ﷺ. Umar ﷺ accepted Islam three days after Hamzah. At that time the Muslims numbered only thirty-nine and Umar brought the number to forty.

"The Prophet ﷺ himself once supplicated to Allah for help by Umar's conversion"

Allah's Messenger ﷺ Gives Umar the Appellation

'al-Farûq'

Umar was eager to call people to Islam publicly. After becoming Muslim, he led Allah's Prophet and his Companions to the Ka'bah to perform prayer in public. The days of preaching Islam in secret were now over!

Until then, Muslims had lived in constant fear of the disbelievers, and most of them kept their faith secret. The time had come to preach the Faith publicly and Allah's Messenger ﷺ gave permission to proclaim Islam openly. The Messenger of Allah ﷺ went out leading two groups of Companions, with Umar at the head of one group and Hamzah at the head of another. They entered the Sacred Mosque and offered their *Salah* in congregation. Allah's Messenger ﷺ led this first public *Salah* in the history of Islam. For this courageous and bold act of Umar, Allah's Messenger ﷺ gave him the title of *al-Farûq*, which means, 'the one who distinguishes between right and wrong'. Muslims could not pray or go round the Ka'bah until Umar accepted Islam. When he entered Islam, he fought the disbelievers until they left the Muslims alone and let them pray.

Umar's *Hijrah* or Emigration to Madinah

When Umar decided to emigrate to Madinah, he did so openly. Everyone migrated in secret, but when Umar decided to migrate, he took a drawn sword in one hand and arrows in another. He put his bow across his shoulders, and went to the Ka'bah. He went around it seven times, and then prayed at the Station of Ibrahâm. He then came to a group of the chiefs of the Quraysh, and said, throwing a challenge at them, 'Whoever would like to see his mother bereaved of a son and his wife lose a husband should face me!' However, none of them moved

from their place. Then he migrated to Madinah boldly.

Umar settled in Madinah and became a sincere advisor to the Messenger of Allah ﷺ. He studied at the hands of the Messenger of Allah ﷺ and learned the Glorious Qur'an and *Sunnah* of the Prophet ﷺ. Umar developed a deep knowledge of the *Sunnah,* which gave him a solid understanding of Islam. He stayed with the Prophet ﷺ and listened to him. When he sat in a gathering with the Prophet ﷺ, he would not leave that gathering until it ended. He was also keen to ask the Prophet ﷺ about any issues that troubled him.

Umar loved the Messenger of Allah ﷺ deeply. He was prepared to sacrifice his life for him.

Activity

Answer the following questions:

1. Why did Umar's ﷺ succession not meet with any resistance?
2. As a leader, what title did Umar adopt? What was its significance?
3. What job did Umar do at an early age? What lessons did it teach him?
4. Why did Umar resist Islam in the beginning?
5. Write a brief note on how Umar accepted Islam.
6. On what occasion did Allah's Messenger ﷺ name Umar 'al-Farūq'?

Fill in the blanks:

1. Umar was one of the few Makkans who were able to ______________ and ______________.
2. As a sportsman, Umar earned a reputation as a ________________.
3. Umar settled in Madinah and became a sincere ______________ to the Prophet ﷺ.

State 'True' or 'False':

1. By profession, Umar was a poet. ___________
2. Umar felt pity for the people travelling to Ethiopia to escape harsh treatment. _______
3. Umar emigrated to Madinah secretly. _________

Umar Participated in all of the Prophet's Battles

Umar Participated in all of the Prophet's Battles

Umar ibn al-Khattab accompanied the Prophet ﷺ in every battle. He was present at Badr, Uhud and all the other battles in which the Messenger of Allah ﷺ participated and did not miss out on a single one of them.

Reinforcements for Iraq: Campaign under Abu Ubayd

The conquests in Iraq during the Caliphate of Abu Bakr, under the leadership of Khâlid ibn al-Walid, mark the first stage of the Islamic conquests that later spread out in the east. During the rule of Umar ibn al-Khattab, there were further victories.

During the time of Abu Bakr, Khalid ibn al-Walid conquered part of the Persian Empire, known as the Kingdom of Hira. Then he was commanded by Abu Bakr to join the expedition in Syria. At the time of his departure, he appointed Muthanna ibn Harithah as the commander of the Muslim army. The Persians were outraged at the loss of Hira, and the emperor sent a huge army under the command of a famous general, Rustom, who was the commander-in-chief of the Persian forces. The Persian forces attacked the places conquered by Muslims and they lost some of them. In view of the growing pressure of the Persians, Muthanna came to Madinah. He asked Umar ibn al-Khattab for reinforcements or additional military support.

It is important to realize that in those days the Islamic state of Madinah did not have a permanent army. There were no salaried, professional soldiers to defend and protect the lands or people. Every Muslim was expected to

be a defender of the Islamic State.

When Abu Bakr died and was buried at night on Tuesday, 22 Jumada al-Âkhirah in the year 13 AH/ 634 CE, the following morning Umar urged the people to fight the people of Iraq. At that time, there was an immense gathering of Muslims in Madinah, who had gathered to take the pledge of loyalty to Umar.

Umar made an urgent proclamation for soldiers to

come forward to fight in the way of Allah. In the beginning, no one responded to the call. Seeing this, Muthanna, still in Madinah, urged them forward in a stirring speech. Inflamed by his words and stung by the reprimand from Umar, men began at last to enlist. The first to come forward was Abu Ubayd, a resident of Tâif; then, following him, greater numbers crowded to the call. When seven thousand soldiers had gathered in this manner, Umar gave the command to Abu Ubayd ibn Mas'ud ath-Thaqafi. This was because he was the first to come forward in eagerness for battle. Umar presented to him the standard, but at the same time, earnestly commanded him to always seek the counsel of the other Companions and include them in governing affairs. Umar ordered Muthanna to hasten before the advance of Abu Ubayd. He re-entered Hira after the absence of a few weeks. A little later, Abu Ubayd too marched forth towards Iraq with a seven-thousand strong army.

"Umar gave the command to Abu Ubayd ibn Mas'ud ath-Thaqafi because he was the first to come forward in eagerness for battle."

The Battle of Namâriq : 13 AH

When Abu Ubayd reached Namâriq, an intense battle took place resulting in the defeat of the Persians, by the Will of Allah. Jabân and Mardânshah, the commanders of the Persian forces, were taken prisoner. They had led the revolt together. Jabân was the right hand of Rustom.

The Battle of Kaskar

In the meantime, Abu Ubayd went after those who had fled the battlefield. They had taken refuge in Kaskar, which was a small town between Kufa and Basra. Abu Ubayd defeated the enemy forces and took over their land. The Muslim army found a large amount of supplies in their stores. Abu Ubayd remained in Kaskar and sent forces to pursue the Persians and discipline the people of the neighbouring towns who had broken the treaty and supported the Persians. The Muslims prevailed after this conquest.

Abu Ubayd's Battle of the Bridge

The defeat of the Persians alarmed Rustom. Enraged at the defeat, he assembled an even larger force under another great warrior, Bahman. The Persians unfurled their royal flag called the 'Great Flag', which was made of panther skin. It was considered lucky by them and was eight cubits wide and twelve cubits long. In addition to this, they sent an array of trained elephants with the army. They reached the place where the Muslims were stationed, and between them was a river that could be crossed by a bridge.

Bahman asked Abu Ubayd whether the Persians should cross the river or the Muslims. The Muslims advised their commander Abu Ubayd, 'Tell them to cross over to us.' He answered, 'They are not braver than we are.'

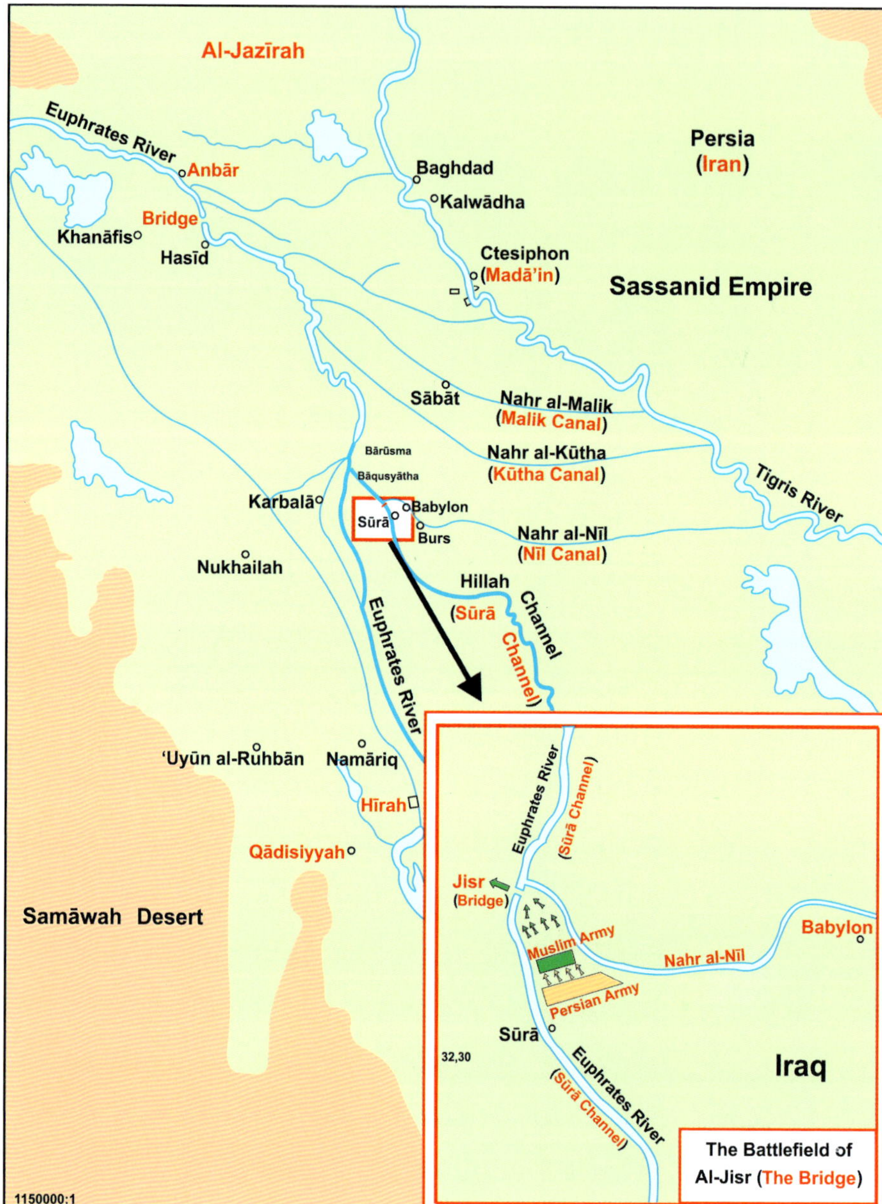

The Battle of Al-Jisr (The Bridge)

Then the Muslim forces crossed over to them and they met in a narrow place, where intense fighting took place. The Muslims had nearly ten thousand soldiers. The

Persians had brought with them an array of elephants. They were wearing many bells to frighten the Muslims' horses. Every time they attacked the Muslims, the horses fled from the elephants because of the sound of those bells. Only a few horses could be made to stand firm, and that too with great difficulty. The Persians targeted the Muslims with arrows and killed many of them. However, the Muslims still managed to kill six thousand of them. Still, the unruly elephants with their jingling bells and frightening trappings spread confusion among the Arab cavalry or mounted troops. The Muslims' horses were frightened of the sound of the bells worn by the elephants and thus, the Muslims could not reach the enemy.

Finally, the riders dismounted and went bravely at the enemy. They tried, with some success, to cut the straps of the litters or saddles, and drive the elephants from the field. It was a hard situation, but the Muslims displayed rare bravery and sacrifice, rarely seen in history. Abu Ubayd urged his men to target the elephants, cut their saddle belts, and push their riders away. Abu Ubayd himself singled out a white elephant with huge tusks. It was the fiercest of them all. He rushed at it, sword in hand. He attacked the white elephant and struck off its trunk with his sword, but the huge beast defended itself with its foreleg, throwing him to the ground and then trampling him to death.

Horror seized the ranks at the shocking spectacle. His brother al-Hakam ibn Mas'ud took the flag and fought the elephant, but he suffered the same fate as Abu Ubayd. The elephant threw him down with its foreleg and stepped on him. One after another, the generals who Abu Ubayd had named to take command in case of disaster were killed, and the troops began to waver. Some Muslim soldiers turned back and crossed the bridge.

In the meantime, a Muslim soldier cut off the ropes that supported the bridge. However, this was not a good idea. Cutting the bridge closed the exit, and panic spread. Many leapt into the swift stream and were drowned. At this critical moment, Muthanna rushed to the front. Backed by a few heroic soldiers, he seized the banner. He called out that he would hold the ground until all the soldiers had passed over. Then he commanded the bridge to be restored, that is, put in good repair. He cried, 'Do not destroy yourselves! Withdraw in order, and I will defend you. Do not rush. Take your time to cross the bridge. We will not leave until we see that you have reached the other side of the river.'

Bahman tried to destroy the remaining Muslim forces, but he was not able to do so. Undoubtedly, the heroes who protected the Muslims until they had withdrawn tried their utmost by standing firm before the enemy. At last, the bridge was restored, five thousand Muslims crossed over, but four thousand were martyred -- either left dead on the field or swept by the flood. A large number of them were Companions of the Prophet ﷺ who had accompanied Abu Ubayd from Madinah. Two thousand of those who withdrew returned to Madinah and elsewhere. Only three thousand Muslim fighters remained with Muthanna.

> "five thousand Muslims crossed over the bridge, but four thousand were martyred - either left dead on the field or swept by the flood."

As for the Persians, six thousand of them were killed. The Persians were plunged into a dire situation. Muthanna withdrew with his remaining troops. He was badly wounded, but he still began his pursuit of the two Persian leaders, Jaban and Mardanshah, in the direction of as-Samâwah. Muthanna pursued them for a long distance. He did not want them to launch a counter-attack, until they had gone far from the place of withdrawal. When he reached as-

A view of Euphrates River

Samâwah, he led a sudden attack with his cavalry, taking the enemy by surprise and defeating them.

Muthanna had lost most of the army. Things, no doubt, looked dark. Still, a hero like Muthanna was not one to despair. His sudden attack stunned the Persians, and they suffered heavy losses as a result. Muthanna managed to capture the two leaders, whom he beheaded. This victory had an immense effect on raising the morale of those who were left of his army, and of the local residents. It also raised the status of Muthanna in the eyes of his troops and the neighbouring tribes. Thus, before long, he regained a firmer footing.

The Battle of Buwaib Ramadan13 AH

Umar ibn al-Khattab calmly received the unhappy tidings of the defeat of the Muslim army. He again appealed to the Muslims in Madinah to go to help their brothers in Iraq. He sent special forces to prepare for war against the Persians. A fresh reinforcement was sent to Muthanna's army.

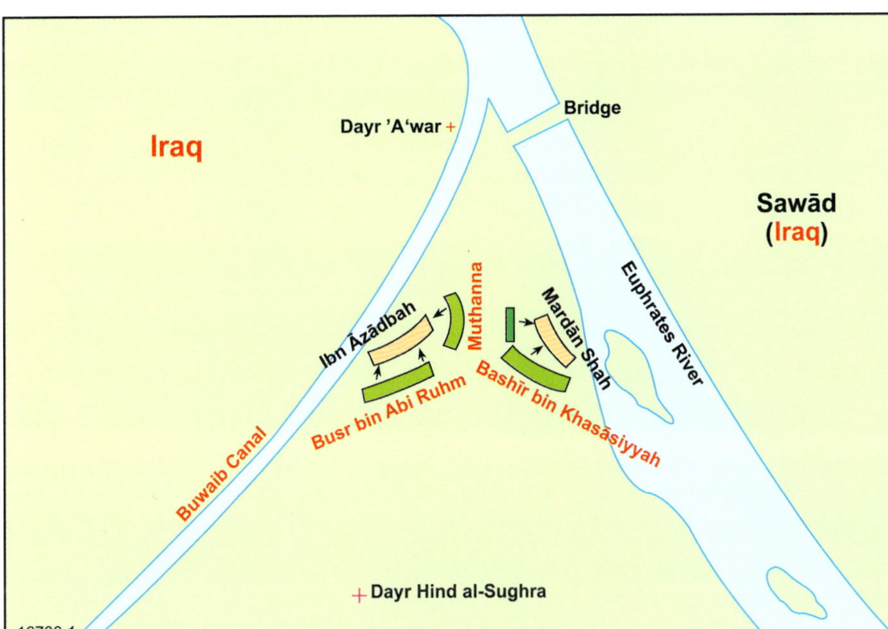

The Battle of Buwaib

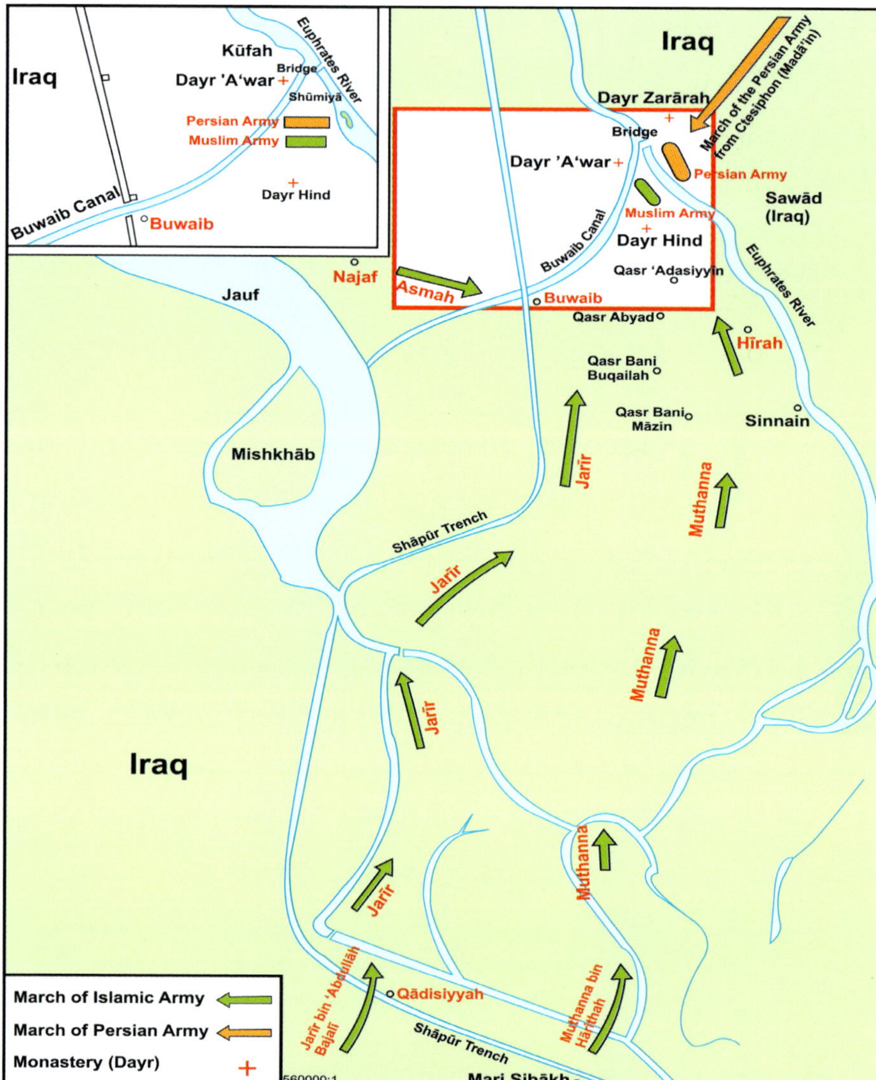

The Battle of Buwaib (1) (Ramadan 13AH / November 634 CE)

The Persians also gathered a huge army. This time, Rustom, the commander-in-chief of the Persian armies, appointed Mahran Hamadani as the commander. Mahran had travelled across Arabia and he knew the Arabian way of fighting. The Muslim army, under the command of

Muthanna, met the Persian at a place called Buwayb, close by where Kufa is situated today. The Muslims invited the Persians to cross the river and they accepted it. The Muslim army was a little more than twenty thousand; while the Persian army, several times larger in number, were about two hundred thousand.

This battle took place in Ramadan 13 AH in which the Muslims fought bravely. After a grim fight, the Persians were defeated. They could not find the way to cross the River Euphrates, because the Muslims destroyed the bridge built by them. There was disorder in the Persian ranks. Mahran, the commander, was killed in the battle. No less than a hundred thousand men lost their lives in the field. As a result of this victory, the entire western region of the Persian Empire fell into the hands of Muslims.

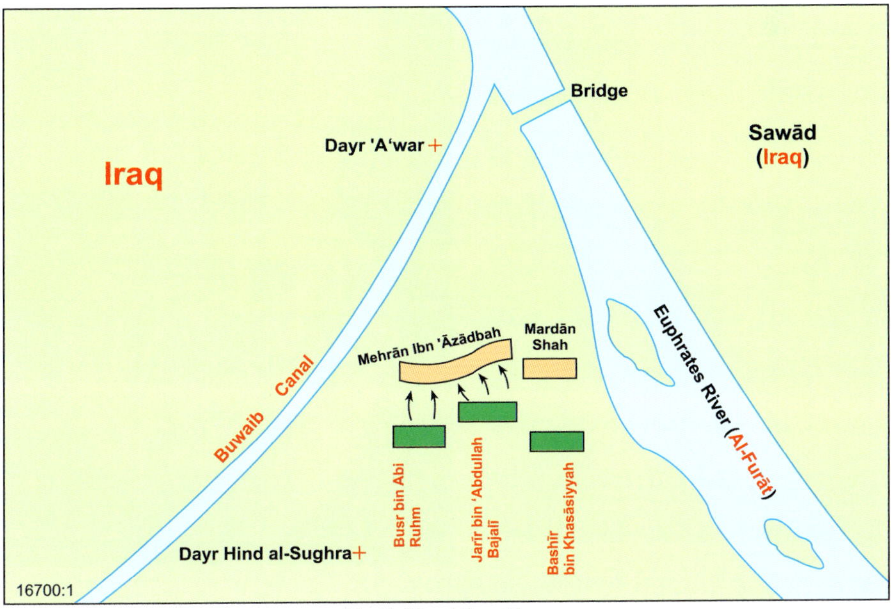

The Battle of Buwaib

The Persian Empire Shaken to its Foundations

The heavy defeat of Buwayb shocked the Persian Empire. It was a cause of great distress not just to the rulers, but to the people as well. For the first time, they felt the strength of the Muslims. The news of the heavy loss of one hundred thousand Persian soldiers and only a few hundred Muslims was received with deep shock and surprise.

At that time, a woman called Puran Dukht was the ruling empress of Persia. People began to say that they had tasted heavy defeats because a weak queen was on the Persian throne. People began to cry out that she was dragging the empire down to ruins. Thus, the empress was immediately dethroned and Yezdgird took her place. He was a

A Statue of Yezdgird

young man who was only twenty-one years old. The new emperor began to reorganize the army, and fortified the frontiers. The nobles rallied around the young emperor loyally and troops were gathered. The people returned to their allegiance. There arose a number of revolts in lands conquered by Muslims and consequently, they lost some of the parts they had conquered earlier once again.

Muthanna sends an urgent message to Umar

Muthanna sent an urgent message to Umar, telling him of the new threats all around. Umar exclaimed, 'I swear by the Lord that I will strike down the proud princes of Persia, with the swords of the princes of Arabia!' He commanded Muthanna to call the border tribes and to withdraw into the frontiers of Arabia. The Muslims were eager to fight, but their commander held them back, obeying Umar's commands and waiting for additional military help. That was in the end of the month of Dhu'l Qa'dah in the year 13 AH/ January 635 CE.

Activity

Answer the following questions:

1. What do you know about the army of the Islamic State of Madinah?
2. Why did Umar give the standard to Abu Ubayd?
3. What role did the elephants play in the Battle of the Bridge?
4. Why did Muthanna go after the two leaders of the Muslim army? How did this incident affect Muthanna?
5. How did the Muslims lose some of the Persian lands that they had conquered earlier?

Match the following:

	A		B	
1	Umar accompanied	a	commander of the Muslim army.	___
2	Rustom was the	b	were to scare the Muslim army.	___
3	Muthanna was the	c	the Prophet ﷺ in every battle.	___
4	The elephant's bells	d	commander of the Persian army.	___
		e	were to scare the Muslims' horses.	___

Complete the following questions:

1. Umar ؓ was the ____________________ of the four Rightly- Guided Caliphs.
2. The royal flag of the Persians was made of ____________________ skin.
3. The Persians could not withdraw during the Battle of Buwayb because ______________.

Chapter 3

Umar's Preparations to Face the Persians

Umar's Preparations to **Face the Persians**

Now Umar issued orders, tougher than ever, for new reinforcements. The command was sent everywhere for the tribes from the south to assemble before the caliph in Madinah. Due to the urgent demand and time being precious, the tribes lying northward were to march straight to Muthanna.

Once this was arranged, Umar set out to perform the Pilgrimage or Hajj. After completing it, he repaired to the camp outside Madinah. He left Ali ibn Abi Talib in charge of Madinah during his absence, and took with him Uthmân ibn Affan and several other prominent Companions of the Messenger of Allah ﷺ. Then, he held a council to consult the Companions about what he was planning to do. There it was debated whether Umar should lead the army to Iraq in person. Finally, it was decided that the Caliph would remain in Madinah. Defeat, if Umar was on the battlefield, might be fatal. On the other hand, if he was stationed in Madinah, he could send column after column against the enemy even in the worst situation.

Iraq and Al-Jazirah

Sa'd ibn Abi Waqqas Appointed as Commander

Soon an army of twenty thousand Muslims was collected. As we have pointed out earlier, Umar himself wanted to lead the army, but the advisory council did not agree to it. The name of Sa'd ibn Abi Waqqas was proposed to lead the army, to which Umar agreed, and Sa'd was appointed as Commander in Iraq. The army consisted of seventy Companions who had earlier participated in the Battle of Badr.

Sa'd ibn Abi Waqqas had embraced Islam in the early days, when he was seventeen years old. He was one of the most intimate Companions of the Prophet ﷺ and had taken part in almost all of the Prophet's ﷺ campaigns. He was also one of the ten to whom Paradise had been announced. He had participated in the great Battle of Badr. He was a brave warrior and a noted archer in the Prophet's ﷺ campaigns. He was the first Muslim to release an arrow in the path of Allah.

As the reinforcements kept coming in, Umar رضي الله عنه sent them one after another to join Sa'd. The number swelled rapidly. In short, Umar left not a single person of any note or dignity in the land, whether warrior, poet, orator, or chief, nor any man who possessed weapons or a mount,

The Roads to Qādisiyyah

but he sent him off to Iraq. Thus reinforced, Sa'd found himself at the head of twenty thousand men. With the column now on its way from Syria, the numbers were over thirty thousand, by far the largest force yet! The army included three hundred Companions in all, who were present during the Pledge of Good Pleasure [*ar-Ridwân*] at al-Hudaybiyyah, while seventy of them had taken part in the Battle of Badr.

Sa'd's Arrival in Iraq and Death of Muthanna

Sa'd marched with his army until he halted in a place called Zarûd: on the pilgrims' route from Iraq. Sa'd began preparing for the decisive battle with the Persians, and waited for the command of the Caliph Umar.

While Sa'd and his army were encamped at Zarûd, Muthanna became gravely ill. In fact, he had never entirely recovered from the wounds received at the Battle of the Bridge. His wounds reopened and began to bleed. He realized that his end was near. As his condition grew worse, he appointed Bashir ibn al-Khasâsiyah to be in charge of those

who were with him, in the event of his death. Muthanna then called his brother Mu'anna and informed him of his last wishes, and asked him to convey them to Sa'd ibn Abi Waqqas. Then Muthanna surrendered his soul to his Creator. The sun that had brightened the Conquests of Iraq had finally set.

> "Muthanna surrendered his soul to his Creator. The sun that had brightened the Conquests of Iraq had finally set."

In his final advice to Sa'd, he told him to fight the enemy of the Muslims [the Persians] on the borders of their land, close to the land of the Arabs. If Allah granted the Muslims victory, they would be able to capture all the land of the enemy, and if the result was otherwise, they would be able to withdraw and be with the other Muslims. Muthanna passed away before Sa'd could reach the appointed place, but he passed on the fruits of his experiences in war against the Persians to the new leader of the war in Iraq.

Until his last breath, Muthanna thought and made plans on behalf of the Muslims and advised Sa'd. When the counsel and suggestions of Muthanna reached Sa'd, he prayed for mercy for him. In fact, Muthanna had left instructions that his wife Salma bint Khasfah should marry Sad ibn Abi Waqqas. Sa'd proposed to her after the completion of her waiting period, and married her. Muthanna wanted to be kind to his wife after he had passed away by letting her marry one of the heroes of Islam, who belonged to the ten Companions who were given the glad tidings of Paradise in their lifetime by the Prophet of Allah ﷺ. Above all, Salma was wise, intelligent and knowledgeable about her husband's strategies in war. In suggesting that his wife marry Sa'd, perhaps Muthanna wanted to benefit the Muslims even after his death.

Muthanna was one of the great generals who secured the triumph of Islam. He possessed great vigour and strategic skill. He was kind-hearted and never used his victory to serve personal ends. It was due to the firm and determined stand that Muthanna took at the Bridge, that the Muslim force was not utterly destroyed there. He always remained loyal to Caliph Umar. In fact, Muthanna was one of the great generals of the world.

Mu'anna, Muthanna's brother, went out to Sa'd, with the sad news of his brother's death. He also delivered Muthanna's dying message to the new commander, advising that the Muslim army should hold their ground on the borders of the desert: 'Fight the enemy there,'

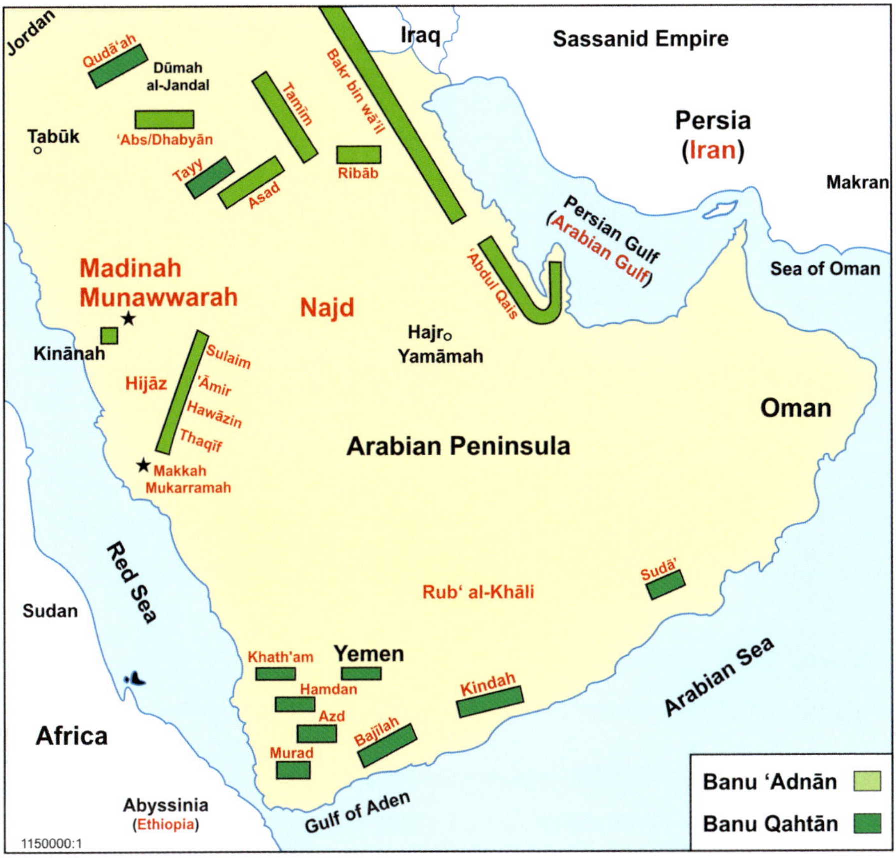

Departure of Tribal Armies from the Arabian Peninsula to Qādisiyyah

were his last words, 'you will be the victors, and even if defeated, you will have the friendly desert behind you. There the Persians would not be able to enter. From there you could return again to the attack.' Sa'd, as he received the message, prayed for the great general. He treated Muthanna's bereaved family with kindness and he discharged his trust. In true Arab tradition, he took Sa'd's widow Salma as wife. Such were the people of that great and pious generation!

Sa'd Encamps at Qadisiyah

Sa'd was in direct contact with Umar all the time, who continually gave instructions about the movement of the army from place to place. The objective of the Muslims was to proclaim Allah's Message: Islam. The sword was used merely to clear the obstacles from the way. It was used to create a leadership where people would be free to accept Islam if they wanted to, which they could not if they were ruled by harsh rulers.

Sa'd organized his troops and marched slowly. Finally, Umar commanded him to encamp at Qadisiyah, a town some 45 kilometres from Kufa. Sa'd advanced to Qadisiyah, set up his headquarters there and waited patiently to observe the movements of the enemy. Meanwhile, Sa'd kept up constant communication with Umar, and wrote to him almost every day.

Umar Asks Sa'd to Send a Delegation

At last, Umar commanded Sa'd to send a delegation to the Persian Emperor to call him and his people to Islam. Charged with this duty, fourteen warriors crossed the plain and presented themselves at the gates of Madâin. It was the capital of the Persian Empire. They were dignified, good-looking men of wisdom and courage. They entered Madâin to meet the Persian Emperor Yezdgird.

An-Nu'man ibn Mûqrin al-Muzani was the leader of the Muslim delegation. Some of the Muslims in the

Great arch of Taq-i Kisr

delegation had fought the Persians and others knew the Persian language.

Yezdgird held his court to receive the delegation. The court was a display of the worldly pomp and glory of the Persian Empire. Yezdgird demanded to know, through an interpreter, 'What motivated you to invade our kingdom?' An-Nu'man spoke on behalf of the delegation, 'Allah showed mercy to us. He sent us a Messenger. He commanded us to do good. He forbade us to do evil. He promised us the good of this world and the Hereafter, if we obeyed him. Embrace Islam; if not, then pay tribute [*Jizyah* or Protection Tax], and you will come under our protection. If you refuse, know that the days of your empire are numbered.' The Emperor replied scornfully, 'If you think you can defeat us, then it is a folly on your part. You are simply nothing, nothing at all, hungry adventurers from a barren land. Come, I will give you a morsel and you shall return

"If you think you can defeat us, then it is a folly on your part. You are simply nothing, nothing at all, hungry adventurers from a barren land..."

full and content.'

One of the delegates replied in strong but modest words, 'You have spoken the truth. Our condition was even worse than that. We were poor and hungry, yet Allah enriched and satisfied us. Allah showed His Mercy and He sent His Prophet to us. Have you chosen the sword? Then, the sword shall decide between us.' The emperor's anger was aroused. He said, 'None of you would have left this place if it were lawful to put ambassadors to death.' Saying this, he ordered for a basketful of earth, and asked, 'Who is the most respectable of you?' Âsim ibn Amr, one of the delegates, stepped forward and said, 'I am the noblest of them.' Yezdgird bade his men to place the basket on Âsim's head. Âsim forthwith seized the load, mounted his charger and bearing it, rode away.

Rustom, the commander-in-chief of the Persian forces, entered the court at that very moment. Yezdgird told him of the insult he had placed upon the simple Arabs. He cried out, 'Simple! It is you who is simple.' He sent people in haste to get the basket back, but it was too late. The horseman was already out of sight. Hastening to Qadisiyah, he placed the load before his commander and exclaimed, 'Rejoice, O Sa'd! Allah has given us the soil of Persia. He has given us the keys to their kingdom.'

Rustom Advances with his Great Army

Rustom now came out with his huge army. Elephants and fighters were gathered from every quarter to swell the forces, now nearly 120,000 strong . The Persian army had thirty-three elephants with them. Rustom travelled with his army until he reached Qadisiyah at a bridge called al-Atiq, facing the Muslim camp, with a river between them. He pitched his camp on the opposite bank of the river.

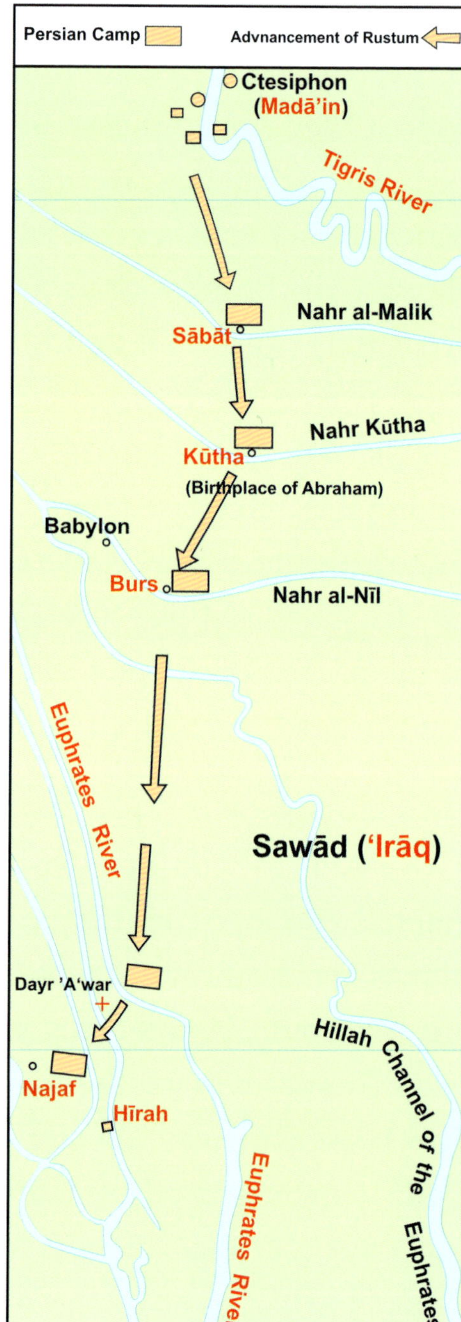

March of Rustum from Madā'in towards Qādisiyyah

Ribei ibn Amir in the Court of Rustom

After camping, Rustom sent word to Sa'd, 'Send us a man so that we may talk to him.' Sa'd sent Ribei ibn Amir. Ribei found Rustom sitting on a throne of gold. Rustom had decorated his court with splendour and pomp. The entire court was carpeted with a cloth of gold. The pillows were of rich silk. A throne studded with precious gems was placed in the centre. Carpets and cushions were interwoven with gold threads. Ribei entered riding his horse. His sword hung in a sheath of cloth. His spear lay tied around with cloth. When he reached the carpets, his horse stepped over them. Then he dismounted and tied the reins of his horse to two pillows. He then advanced forward, taking support of his spear, piercing into the carpet and cutting holes in it.

> "We do not stand in need of your carpets. The earth spread by Allah Most High is enough for us."

The courtiers tried to take his

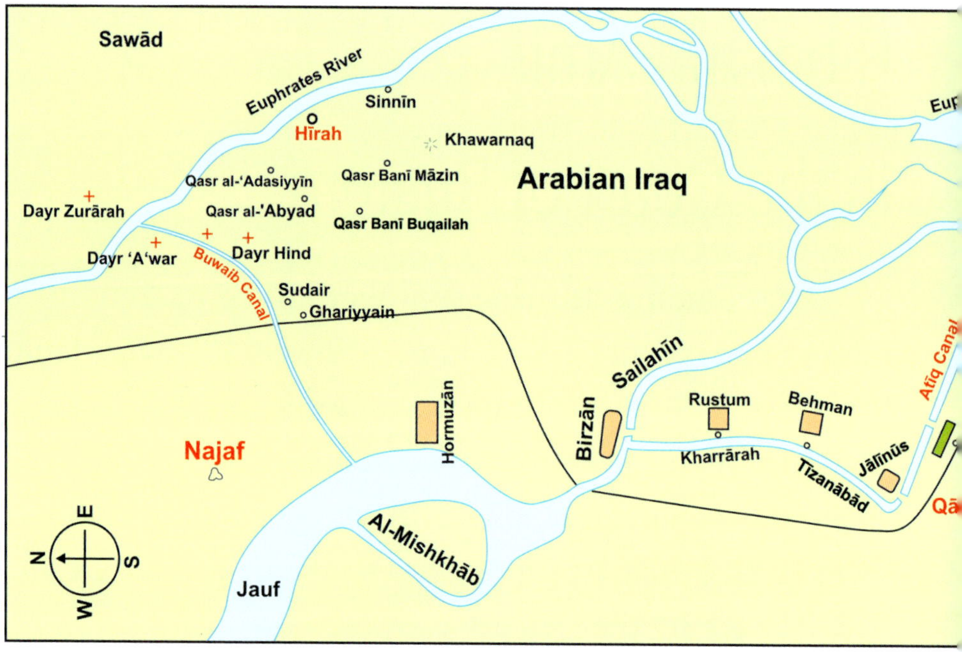

Rustum and his army near Qādisiyyah

weapons away from him. Thereupon, Ribei thundered, 'I have come upon your invitation, and not on my own.' Rustom asked them to leave him alone. Ribei then stuck his spear into the carpet. He slit a portion of the carpet with his dagger and sat down on the earth and said, addressing Rustom, 'We do not stand in need of your carpets. The earth spread by Allah Most High is enough for us.' Rustom then asked Ribei, through an interpreter, 'What is your purpose in waging war against us?' Ribei answered, 'We intend to bring the slaves of Allah into the vastness of the next world from the narrowness of this world. We want to promote justice. We want to bring Islam in place of cruelties and false religions. Anyone who embraces Islam, we will not interfere with his wealth, property, or country. But we shall fight whoever stands in our way until we go either to Paradise or gain victory.'

Rustom then said, 'We have heard what you said. How much time can you give me to think about it?' Ribei said, 'Three days only.' The firmness and presence of mind of Ribei left Rustom and his courtiers astonished. He consulted with his courtiers, but they refused to enter into any peace agreement with the Muslims. Three days' grace period was over. Rustom could no longer delay now. He ordered his troops to get ready for battle at once. The Muslims were fully prepared for the fight. Sa'd ibn Abi Waqqas ordered the reciters of the Qur'an to read *Sûrah al-Anfâl* [*Sûrah* eight of the Qur'an]. Following this, a feeling of calm descended upon them. The people offered *Dhuhr* prayer and Sa'd commanded his army to advance.

> "How much time can you give me to think about it?' Ribei said, 'Three days only."

Activity

Answer the following questions:

1. What was the wisdom in Umar not taking part in the battle in person?
2. Mention a few qualities of Sa'd ibn Abi Waqqas.
3. Why did Muthanna advise Sa'd to fight close to the lands of the Arabs?
4. What did Āsim tell Sa'd, when he placed the basket of earth in front of him?
5. What was the main purpose of the Muslims behind attacking Persia?

Fill in the blanks:

1. When Umar decided not to go, ____________________ was appointed as the commander of the army in Iraq.
2. The army led by Sa'd consisted of ____________________ men, the largest force by far.
3. Muthanna was one of the ________________ generals of the world.
4. The Muslims gave a grace period of ________________ days to Rustom.

Refer to Context

1. '…I will strike down… with the swords of the princes of Arabia.'
2. '…we were poor and hungry and Allah satisfied us.'

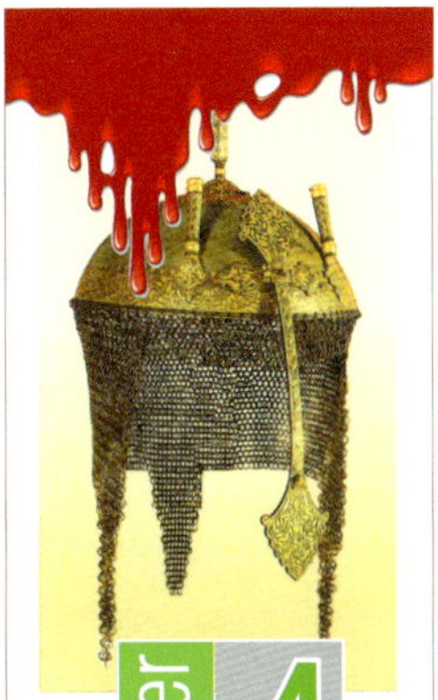

Chapter 4

The Battle of Qadisiyah

The Battle of Qadisiyah

At last, the armies stood face to face. Rustom had no more excuses for putting off the decisive day. Three days' grace, according to the tradition of the Prophet of Allah ﷺ, was given and was over. The battle lasted for four days. Sa'd ibn Abi Waqqas was suffering from sciatica [pain in the back, hip, and outer side of the leg, caused by pressure on the sciatic nerve].

Moreover he had boils, which made him unable to ride or sit. So he lay on his chest on a pillow, looking over the battlefield from a fort which was situated in Qadisiyah; from where he sent orders written on pieces of paper. The heroic feats of Badr were re-enacted on the battlefield.

The fighting was severe and the bloodshed was great. The elephants were the terror of the Arabs. They threatened to paralyse their efforts. Sa'd soon learnt that the eye and trunk were the only parts of the elephants that made them helpless or open to attack. He ordered, 'Aim at these and we shall be rid of this calamity.' There were two huge elephants that were the leaders of the herd. One of the Muslim warriors dismounted, and advancing boldly, he thrust his lance into the eye of the great white elephant. Smarting at the pain, it shook its head in fear and pain, threw its rider to the ground and swayed its trunk to and fro. The other

Islamic and Persian armies before the battle

fared even worse. They pierced both its eyes, and slashed its trunk. Uttering a shrill scream of pain, the blinded and maddened beast darted forward on the Muslim ranks.

Shouts and spears drove it back upon the Persians. It kept rushing wildly to and fro between the armies, and followed at last by the other elephants, it charged right into the Persian ranks. Thus the whole herd of huge elephants, their trunks high, trumpeting as they raced and trampling all before them plunged into the river and vanished on the distant shore. For

Pursuit of the Persian fugitives after the Battle of Qādisiyyah

the moment, the din and bustle of war was quieted as both armies stared at the threatening sight. The Persian wings began to waver. A fierce Muslim attack shook their centre. It opened and laid bare the shore with Rustom on his throne. He had barely time to escape. He took shelter beneath a mule, but a chance blow by a rushing soldier brought down the animal. It fell on Rustom and crushed his back. He crawled into the river, but he was recognized by a Muslim warrior who grabbed him by his leg, drew him out and slew him. He then mounted Rustom's throne and proclaimed, 'I have killed Rustom!'

The main body of the Persians fled. No sooner was their Commander slain, than rout and bloodshed began. To the right and left, up the riverbank and down, Muslim fighters chased the Persians relentlessly. The plain, far and wide, was strewn with dead soldiers.

The Persians numbered some one hundred and twenty thousand warriors. The Muslim soldiers were about thirty thousand. The Muslim loss far exceeded that of any previous engagement. In all, 8500 Muslim fighters were martyred. The number of Persians killed was thirty thousand, and the battle ended. This took place in the month of Shâbân in the year 15 AH/ 636 CE.

Good News

of the Victory Reaches Umar

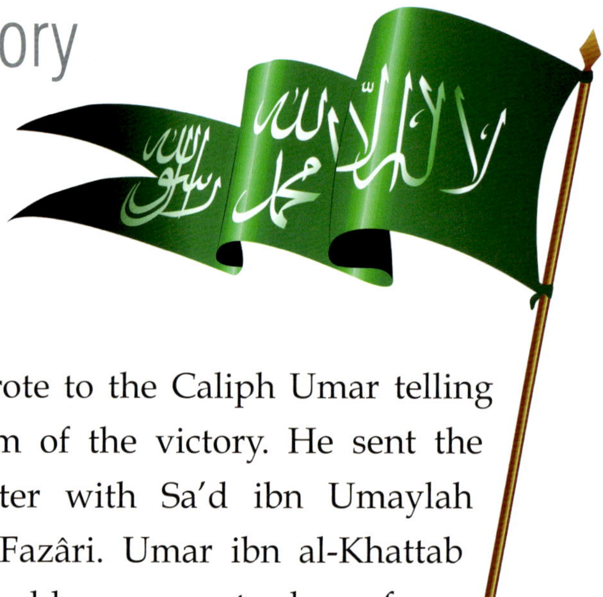

Sa'd wrote to the Caliph Umar telling him of the victory. He sent the letter with Sa'd ibn Umaylah al-Fazâri. Umar ibn al-Khattab would come out alone from the gates of Madinah early in the morning to see if some messenger was coming from Qadisiyah. He would wait from morning until midday and then return home.

At last, a camel rider arrived outside the city, who replied to Umar's question on news from Qadisiyyah shortly, 'Allah has defeated the enemy.' Unrecognized, Umar followed the bringer of good news on foot. He asked him questions about the great battle. Entering Madinah, people crowded round the Caliph. After greeting him, they began to congratulate him upon the victory. The messenger, embarrassed, cried out, 'Why did you not tell me that you were the Commander of the Faithful (Amîr al-Mu'minîn)?' Umar answered, 'It is just as well. Don't worry about it, my brother!' Umar was deeply interested and concerned about the Muslims. He had a great sense of responsibility and was deeply humble. He did not mind running alongside the rider, asking him for news of the battle as the messenger was duty-bound. He was required to deliver the news to the caliph first. He did not realize that the man running after him on foot was the caliph himself, until he learnt it from the people of Madinah. This displays the great character and attitude of Umar ibn al-Khattab. The Muslims are rightly entitled to take pride in him before the entire world.

For the enemy, the defeat was fateful and decisive. In fact, the Battle of Qadisiyah was one of the most

Zoroastrians' Tower of Silence. Yazd, Iran

decisive battles in the history of the world. As a result, the gates of Iraq and from there, all of Persia or Iran were opened. After that, the Muslim victories came one after another. Islam spread throughout Persia and beyond.

In Qadisiyah, the Muslims dealt a blow to the Persians from which they could never recover. Most of the people of Persia and Iraq at that time were either Zoroastrians or Christians. The Muslims did not force them to change their religion. On the contrary, the Muslims convinced the local population of the beauty of Islam by their ideal behaviour and fair treatment of the people. Over the years, most of the Persians and Iraqis accepted Islam.

The Eastern Roman Empire

We had left Khalid ibn al-Walid in Syria. We have already discussed the causes of war between the Romans (sometimes called Byzantines). During the time of the Caliph Abu Bakr, the Muslims had defeated the Romans on the Syrian front and conquered a number of cities like Basra and Ajnadayn. They laid siege to Damascus when Abu Bakr died. After his death, they conquered Damascus, Hims, and Qansarin. In all these three battles, Khalid ibn al-Walid played a very significant role. Umar ibn al-Khattab said, 'May Allah bless the soul of Abu Bakr! He set Khalid in the right place.'

The fall of some important cities angered the Roman Emperor, Heraclius. He sent a huge army to fight against the Muslims. In order to face this formidable force, Muslims left some of the regions conquered by them, and returned to secure borders. While leaving the conquered

Panorama detail with Umayyad mosque in Aleppo, Syri

places, the Islamic forces paid back the protection tax or *Jizyah* they had collected from the non-Muslim dwellers of those regions, telling them, 'Since we cannot protect you, we are returning it.' This was an extremely rare example of integrity set by Muslims in history. The people of those regions were greatly impressed by the Muslims' fair dealings.

The Conquest of **Damascus, Syria**

The conquests in Syria during the reign of Umar ibn al-Khattab represent the second stage of conquests in this direction, after the conquests at the time of Abu Bakr as-Siddiq. In fact, Damascus was the seat of the Roman Empire. It was their fortress. It was considered the 'Queen of Cities'. The number of Roman troops in Damascus was 60,000. There was the possibility of an additional 20,000 coming from Hims. Moreover, there were 40,000 soldiers ready to step in. The Romans chose to stay in Damascus due to its built-up defences, walls, and forts. They expected extra military help to come from outside to engage the Muslim troops. The commander-in-chief of the Roman troops was the Emperor Heraclius himself.

The size of the Muslim army that lay siege was approximately 20,000 men. The rest of the forces were placed in Fihl to guard that direction. When necessary, these troops in Fihl could be called back to support the siege. The Muslim army was highly organized. Its morale was very high.

Damascus was a great city and an important commercial centre. It was fortified and surrounded by strong walls built of stones, 20 feet high and 10 feet wide. Heraclius had increased its defence after the Persian invasion of this land. Its gates were kept firmly closed. The city walls were

Ancient Roman time town in Palmyra (Tadmor), Syria. Greco-Roman & Persian Period

surrounded by a ten feet wide trench. The waters of the Barada River flowed into it. Thus, Damascus had become a fortified castle, which could not easily be broken through. This shows that the Roman defence of Damascus was very strong. These fortifications forced the Muslim army not to attempt to breach the city of Damascus. Therefore, the Muslim army placed the city under a state of siege.

The commander of operations in Syria was Abu Ubaydah ibn al-Jarrah. The siege of Damascus lasted for seventy days. It was a very harsh siege. Heavy weapons such as catapults were used. Khalid ibn al-Walid was stationed in the central part of the city and commanded the troops at the eastern gate of the city.

The Romans thought the Muslims would not be able to keep up such a long siege, especially in winter. However, the Muslims were men of deep faith and had great patience. They were quite able to withstand the changes in weather. The Muslim commanders let the soldiers take over abandoned churches and houses in the fertile district called al-Ghûla. The troops relaxed there. They took turns on a weekly basis. Thus, the troops at the gates changed places periodically. Hence, the siege could virtually continue indefinitely.

Besides, the Muslims did not stop here. They continued

to study ways and means to overcome the Roman defensive shield. Khalid was finally able to select a suitable place for crossing the hurdles and entering the city of Damascus. He chose a place that was filled with water and most difficult to cross. He prepared rope ladders for climbing the walls, and waited patiently for a suitable opportunity.

On a certain day, the Roman governor organised a feast for the soldiers defending the city. They ate and drank, relaxing in merriment and began to leave their posts. Khalid ibn al-Walid knew of the festivities, for nothing escaped his vigilant eye. He neither slept himself, nor let others fall asleep. Thus, counting upon the break in festivities, he decided to seize it as the occasion for a general assault. The Roman defences on Khalid's side were by far the most frightening: the moat was deeper, and the walls were stronger, but the troops at the spot were less on the alert than elsewhere. In their negligence, Khalid found his opportunity. As evening settled in, Khalid readied his soldiers and took with him al-Qa'qa ibn Amr and Math'ur ibn Adi. He told the rest of the troops: 'If you hear the *Takbir* [*Allahu Akbar*: the battle cry] from the top of the walls, then come to our help and head towards the gate.'

In the darkness before dawn, they stealthily crossed the deep water-filled moat upon air-filled skins. They reached the city-walls and threw their rope ladders onto the high wide walls. The rope ladders were fitted with solid hooks on the ends to be fixed to the walls and carry the weight of the climbers. Two of these hooks were firmly planted on the wall. Qa'qa and Ma'thur climbed up the wall and planted the other rope ladders and their hooks. In this way, all the rope ladders were arranged to help the first wave of invaders. The first wave, which had now increased in numbers, descended the walls near the gates. Thus, the way was quietly secured, while others scaled rapidly. Right and left, they surprised the napping Roman soldiers and put them to the sword.

The gate from within was forced open, and the appointed battle cry *'Allahu-Akbar!'* resounded from the walls to the waiting troops outside. Panic stricken, the Roman soldiers fled from the attackers, and Khalid's columns poured in through the gateway, heading towards the city from this direction. In this way, the Muslim army entered the city of Damascus and this magnificent city, 'the Eye of the East', passed from the grip of Heraclius into the hands of Caliph Umar ibn al-Khattab. This took place in the year 14 AH/ 633 CE. The loss of Damascus alarmed the Romans. As the superpower of its time, the Roman Empire had not considered the rise of Islam a serious threat to their power in Syria.

Applying Some Clever Military Strategies

During the conquest of Damascus, the Muslims made use of extremely clever military strategies. They used elements of surprise, aggression, seizing opportunities and creativity on the part of the field commanders. This is obvious in how Khalid sent out scouts and looked for the best place to breach the walls, and how that siege affected the situation and changed the siege into an attack.

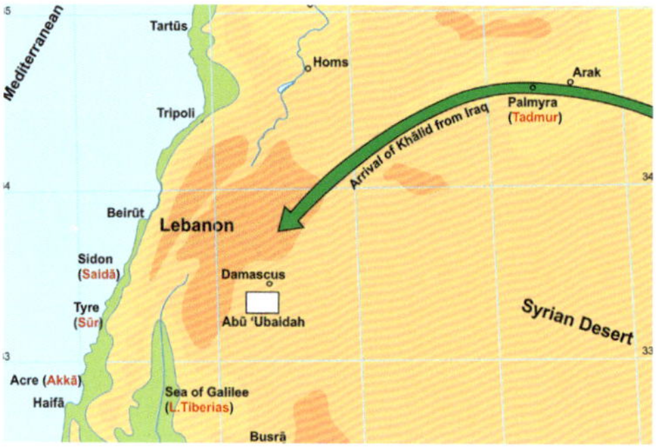

If we compare what Khalid ibn al-Walid did, using rope-ladders to climb the walls of Damascus, with what the Egyptian army did in the October war of 1973 CE, when they crossed Israel's Bar-Lev Lane, making use of rope-ladders to reach the enemy's defense positions, we realize that it was an exact copy in style and method, of the battle strategy adopted by Khalid ibn al-Walid. Islamic conquests display the genius of the Muslims and prove that present day battles draw a lot from the creative military brilliance of Muslims in the past.

Activity

1. When did the Battle of Qadisiyah take place?
2. Why was Sa'd unable to physically take part in the Battle of Qadisiyah?
3. How did the Muslims deal with the elephants?
4. Why did the Muslims return the *Jizyah*?
5. How do you know that Damascus was a well-forti fied city?
6. How did Khalid ibn al-Walid use the Romans' celebration to attack them?

1. The heroic feats of ____________ were re-enacted on the battlefield of Qadisiyah.
2. The _____________ and ________________ were the only two vulnerable parts of the elephant.
3. To deal with the harsh weather conditions, Muslims took over abandoned _____________ and ________________, and turns took resting in them.
4. As powerful as the Roman Empire was, it did not consider the rise of ____________ as a serious threat.

1. 'It is well. Don't worry about it, my brother.'

Chapter 5

Conquest of Jerusalem

[16 AH/ 637 CE]

Conquest of Jerusalem

[16 AH/ 637 CE]

In those days, Romans also ruled Palestine and Egypt. Palestine was a part of the province of Syria, while Egypt was a separate province. Palestine was governed by a Roman commander called Artabun. He was the guardian of Jerusalem with part of his army. He was second in authority only to the Emperor himself.

The Muslims had spiritual links to Jerusalem. Several Prophets and Messengers of Allah had lived in that land and were buried in or around Jerusalem. On the Night of Isrâ and Mi'raj, Allah's Messenger ﷺ was first taken to Jerusalem [*Bayt al-Maqdis* or *al-Quds*]. Before migration to Madinah, and during their early days in Madinah, Muslims used to pray facing Jerusalem.

Artabun had placed two huge number of troops in Ramallah [north of Jerusalem] and in Jerusalem itself. Artabun was considered the wisest, most skilful, shrewd and effective Roman commander of his time. Amr bin al-Âs was leading the army in front of Jerusalem. After the capture of some other key Roman cities, Abu Ubaydah and Khalid ibn al-Walid also joined him.

Amr bin al-Âs wrote to Umar about the situation, seeking his advice and further orders. Umar wrote back his famous sentence, 'We are going to pit our Artabun against their Artabun. Let us see who wins.' What he meant was that both the leaders were the wisest in opened access to Palestine and paved the way for the conquest of Jerusalem.

Ramallah was just eighteen miles from Jerusalem. Artabun himself commanded the Jerusalem wing of the troops. The troops at Ramallah were in command of another commander called Tazariq. Finally, the Muslims laid a tight siege to the Holy City under the command of

Amr bin al-Âs. The city was well fortified. The fighting began after a three-day siege. When the Muslims advanced towards the walls, the Roman troops rained down arrows upon them. They protected themselves with their shields. The siege went on for four months. There was no day on which fierce fighting did not take place. The Muslims had to endure rain, snow and bitter cold. Finally, the Romans gave up all hope of further resistance. However, Artabun said, 'The one who will conquer Jerusalem will be a man whose name is Umar.' Amr bin al-Âs wrote to Umar who was in Madinah. He informed him, 'Artabun does not believe anyone would conquer the city except you. I have been fighting a fierce battle, but it seems the final honours are saved for you! What do you say?'

So, Umar, after consultation, set out for Syria with reinforcements, leaving Ali ibn Abi Talib in charge of

Madinah in his stead. He camped at a place called Jâbiyah, where the people of Jerusalem came to him and pleaded for peace. They made a treaty with him on the basis that they would pay the *Jizyah*: the protection tax. This is how Jerusalem was conquered.

Text of the Jerusalem Pact

The peace treaty that Umar signed clearly shows that Islam is a peace-loving religion. It does not force others to believe what they do not want to. It also clearly shows that the Muslims dealt with the Christians present in Jerusalem in a manner, which they did not expect. This is because the conquerors were known to force whatever they willed on the conquered. However, this was not the case with Umar ibn al-Khattab. He stood for Islam and did not do anything of the sort.

Islam does not force anyone to enter its fold. It does not accept the Faith of anyone who does not believe in it out of his own free will. Faith is not something that can be imposed on people. Faith is the action of the heart. And no one knows what is in the heart, except Allah Most High. A person may pose as someone who believes while he really does not. Hence, Muslims have always given people the freedom of worship. They protected them if they chose

> Faith is not something that can be imposed on people. Faith is the action of the heart.

to live under Muslim rule and paid protection by paying the *Jizyah* or protection tax. Living under Muslim rule and justice offered them a peaceful life. It gave the non-Muslims an opportunity to see at close hand the beauty, tolerance, fair treatment and justice of Islam. It gave them an opportunity to experience the reality of Islam. This led masses of people to embrace Islam, as it happened in all the countries conquered by Muslims.

Conquest of Egypt & Libya

The Roman Empire had a strong base of the Roman navy at Alexandria, Egypt. The Roman Empire was still considered a power. Hence, Egypt was a grave danger to the security of Arabia. The Romans were busy scheming against the Muslims. They were trying to regain the

View of Alexandria harbor, Egypt

territories conquered by the Muslims and to attack them through Egypt. It was, therefore, necessary from the point of view of defence to drive the Romans from Egypt. Above all, the Muslims had a faith, a religion, which they wanted to establish all over the world. Egypt bordered Palestine and therefore, it was natural for the Muslims to flow into Egypt after having conquered Palestine.

By conquering Syria, the Muslims successfully divided the Roman Empire into two halves. The only connection between them was now the sea. Besides, Egypt was the

The fortress in Alexandria, Egypt

granary of the Romans, which provided them with food supplies. Alexandria was an important city for the Romans. It was their seat of commerce and trade. A fleet of ships were stationed in its safe and spacious harbour from where communication was maintained with all the seaports of the Empire. The overflowing produce of well-watered fields fed the great cities of the Roman Empire. The common people, ground down by oppression, were ever ready to rise against their rulers.

All this led Amr bin al-Âs [the commander of the Persian expedition] to conclude that the Romans would not stand a chance to face the Muslim invasion of Egypt. If it were left under Roman control, it would pose a constant threat to the Muslim state. Consequently, the conquest of Egypt was a part of the plan already drawn by the Caliph, Umar ibn al-Khattab. Ultimately, he gave Amr bin al-Aas the necessary permission to lead an expedition against Egypt. Umar appointed him as its governor if Allah enabled him to conquer Egypt. He sent az-Zubayr bin al-Awwam after him with reinforcements. The number of the reinforcements Umar sent to Egypt reached twelve thousand. Thus, it is proven beyond doubt that Umar personally ordered the invasion of Egypt.

Market at Leptis Magna Libya (Roman Empire)

Route of the Conquest

In the year 18 A.H. [639 CE], Amr bin al-Âs launched his attack across the Sinai Peninsula starting from Palestine, and advanced without serious resistance up to the fortress of Babylon [to the South of Modern Cairo at the apex of the Delta].

In fact, the conquest of Egypt is considered the third stage in the conquests of the major regions of the Roman Empire. Amr bin al-Âs marched toward Egypt along the coast. He went from Rafah [the border between Gaza-Palestine and Sinai], to

Attack on Egypt from Palestine

Roman ruins in Coptic Christian city area in Cairo Egypt

Arish to Pelusium (an ancient city on the river Nile) and continued to advance toward Cairo, and then Alexandria. This shows the military skills of Amr bin al-Aas. He may have taken this route either because it was relatively lightly defended as compared to the heavy Roman presence in Syria or because the route was familiar to him,.

The course of the Egyptian conquests were as follows:

The Conquest of Pelusium

As Amr headed westwards, he did not encounter any Roman army before reaching Pelusium. The Romans had fortified Pelusium to check the Muslims; relying on their famed defence and siege skills.

The Muslims laid a tight siege to the city, while the Romans remained firmly resolved. This prolonged the siege to several months. One day, a Roman unit came out to fight the Muslims, but they were beaten back and forced to flee. The Muslims chased them as they were making their way back to the fortress-city. The Muslims managed to reach the gate before the Romans could enter. The first Muslim to enter the city was Asmiqa. This led the way to a resounding victory for the Muslims. The Copts present in the city helped the Muslims and informed them about the weaknesses and soft targets in the city's defences. After their successful entry, the Muslims pulled down walls and fortifications so that the Romans would not be able to benefit from them in the event of their return. Then Amr advanced, meeting with only a little resistance, until he came to Bilbeis.

The Conquest of Bilbeis

Near Bilbeis [an ancient city on the Nile Delta], the Romans came out with a large force. They wanted to stop the Muslim advance towards the castle at Babylon, near modern-day Cairo. The Romans sent two ambassadors to Muslims. Amr called them to Islam, and offered them the option to pay the *Jizyah* or the Protection Tax if they did not want to embrace Islam. These two ambassadors went back to Muqawqis, the ruler of Egypt, and Artabun, the Roman governor. They told them what the Muslims wanted, but Artabun refused and insisted on fighting. The Muslims defeated him and drove him and his troops back to Alexandria.

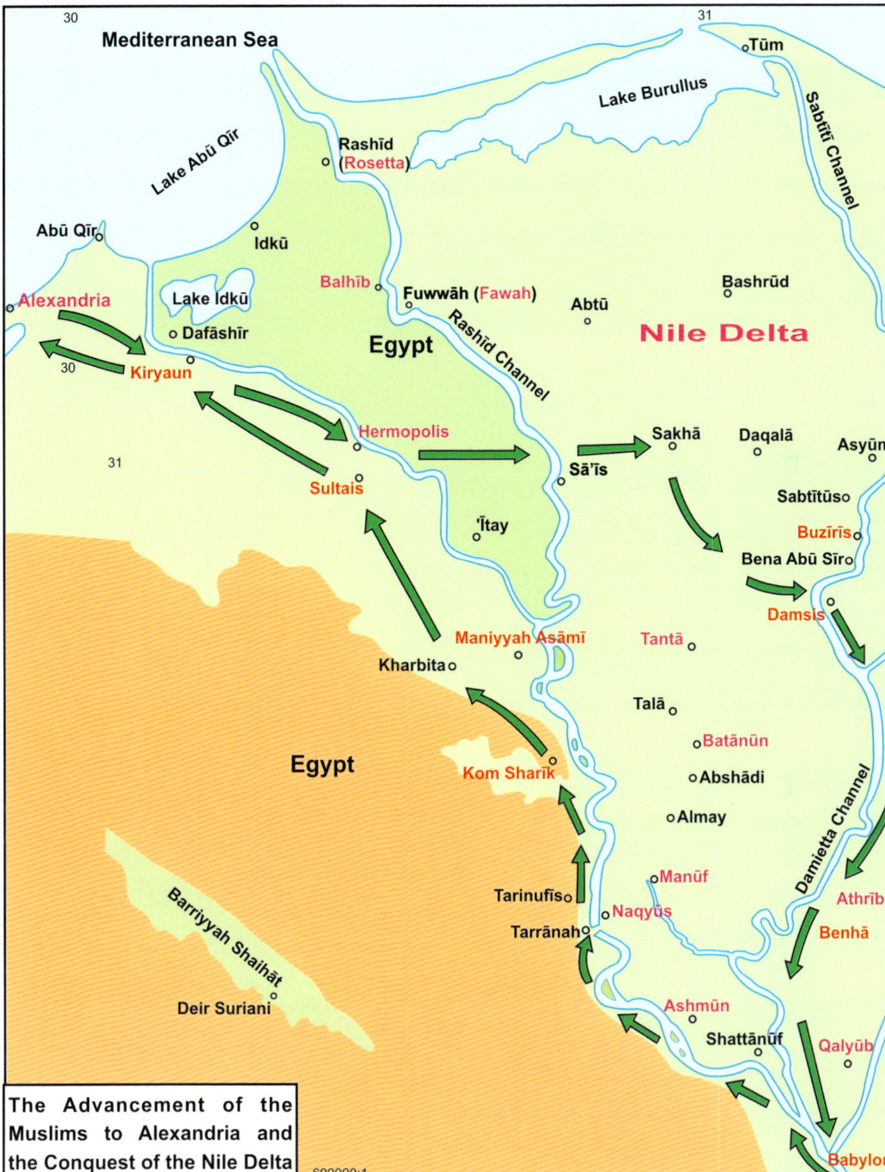

The Advancement of the Muslims to Alexandria and the Conquest of the Nile Delta

A remarkable incident took place here, which is worth mentioning. When Bilbeis was conquered, the Muslim army found the daughter of Muqawqis called Armanosa among the inhabitants. She was very dear to her father and was being forced to marry Constantine, the son of Heraclius, the Roman Emperor. She was not willing to marry him. She, therefore, had taken refuge in the city along with her lady-in-waiting, Barbara. The Muslim army was soon able to take many of her slaves into captivity.

Amr bin al-Âs told the troops, 'Muqawqis had sent a present to the Prophet ﷺ. I think we should send his daughter and her female slaves and courtiers back to him along with whatever wealth we seized from them.' The council agreed to his proposal. Hence, Amr sent her back to her father respectfully, with all her belongings. Her father was very pleased to have her back and with the Muslim behaviour in this matter.

The Conquest of Umm Danin

After the conquest of Bilbeis, Amr marched forward for a month till he reached Umm Danin, also known as Maxus, a village north of Babylon. It is situated on the river Nile. The Muslims fought a major battle around the city. Amr requested Umar ibn al-Khattab for help, to which he responded by sending a four-thousand-man brigade. It is said that

a man with a thousand more men, in terms of mettle and courage, commanded each thousand of this reinforcement. Umar said in his message, 'Know that you have now twelve thousand more men with you and twelve thousand cannot be defeated due to lack of numbers.'

The Romans and their Copt allies came out to face the Muslims and a fierce battle took place. Amr applied the genius battle skills developed by Khalid bin al-Walid by dividing his forces into three divisions. The enemy was defeated, but some of them managed to find safety in the castle of Babylon.

Battle at the Castle of Babylon

Amr took his army now to the castle of Babylon, and laid a tight siege to it, which lasted for seven months. As the siege dragged on, az-Zubair bin al-Awwam announced, 'I offer my life to Allah. By this, I hope Allah will grant victory to the Muslims.'

At night, the Muslims scaled the walls and engaged the enemy inside the castle in a savage fight. The first man to drop inside the castle was az-Zubair. He was with a thousand soldiers in terms of their superior mettle and courage. He had placed a ladder on the wall near the public bath. He climbed it and told the Muslims to storm the castle on hearing the battle cry of *Allahu Akbar*. Thus, when he sounded the cry, it was repeated by the Muslims outside the fort. It resounded with a deafening effect, to such an extent that the enemy thought that the entire Muslim army had managed to slip into the fort. This led the enemy to run helter-skelter. Meanwhile az-Zubair and his troops headed for the castle gate and threw it open for their brethren outside. Hence, the Muslims conquered the city by force. Later, the Muslims destroyed the city's built-up defences, which consisted of towers and walls in order to make them useless for the enemy.

Conquest of Alexandria

Amr stayed at Babylon for several months. He wanted to give his army a chance to get back on their feet and

Mosque of Abu Abbas al Mursi in Alexandria, Egyp

awaited permission from the Caliph to advance towards Alexandria. When the order arrived, he placed a strong force at Babylon and marched with the rest of his army toward their next target in the year 21 AH/ May, 641 CE.

A team of Copts, who were now sure that their best interests lay in helping the Muslim forces, also went out with his army. They paved the roads and built bridges and markets for the Muslims. The Copts, therefore, now allied to the Muslim cause. At last, Amr presented himself with his troops before the city walls of Alexandria. It was a formidable fortress. The Muslims shot their artillery consisting of arrows and darts at the enemy. The enemy fled in their ships. The Muslims shot at the enemy navy and chased them in the river.

It is important to note that at the time of the Muslim conquest of Alexandria, it was the capital of the region. It was also the financial capital and the Romans were keenly aware of the dangers posed by the Muslim invasion of the city. So concerned were they that Heraclius, the Roman Emperor himself went on to say, 'If the Muslims conquer Alexandria, that would spell the end of the kingdom of Romans and mark their end.' It is narrated that Heraclius wished to personally face the Muslims in the battle for Alexandria, but Allah caused his death during the siege. After the death of Heraclius, the Roman Empire was beset with infighting and disorder.

The siege of Alexandria dragged on for many months. This led Amr bin al-Âs to fear that his troops would be exhausted and their confidence would be shaken. Ultimately, Amr bin al-Âs placed the troops under the command of Ubadah bin Samit, and the Muslims conquered Alexandria the same day. Thus after a continuous siege of nine months, Alexandria was conquered in the last month of the year 21 AH/ November, 641 CE.

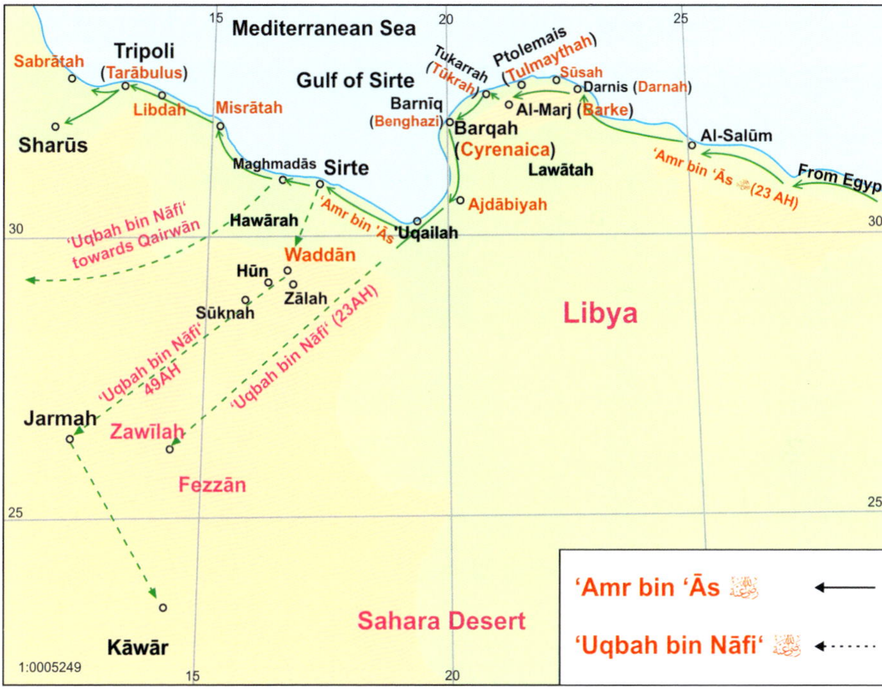

Conquests of Barqah (Libya) and Tripoli

The Conquest of Barca and Tripoli [Libya]

After consolidating the conquest of Egypt, Amr set out to continue his advance westwards as the Romans had troops in Barca and Tripoli. This took place in the year 22 AH/ 642 CE. The road between Alexandria and Barca at that time was filled with granaries and buildings. Amr did not encounter any fighting along this route. When he reached Barca, he made a peace treaty with its people. After that, he marched towards Tripoli, which was strongly fortified and held a huge Roman force. They shut its gates and laid a siege which lasted for four months. Finally, the Muslim troops conquered it.

Libya Tripoli Leptis Magna Roman archaeological site
Arch of Septimus Severus Unesco World Heritage Site

Thus, the Muslim state during the reign of Umar covered a huge portion of the globe. The Rivers Oxus and the Indus in the East; West Africa and its desert in the West defined its boundaries, the mountain ranges of Asia Minor and Armenia in the North; and the Nubian State and Pacific Ocean in the South.

Activity

Answer the following questions:

1. What significance did the Holy city of Jerusalem have for Muslims?
2. Why did Umar himself go to Jerusalem?
3. How does the 'Jerusalem Pact' prove that Islam is a peace-loving religion?
4. Give reasons why conquering Egypt was a practical move.
5. Why did Amr take the route he took?

Fill in the blanks:

1. ______________________ was an important city for the Romans.
2. Non-Muslims lived safely under the Muslim rule by paying ____________________.

Refer to Context:

1. 'We are going to pit our Artabun against their Artabun.'
2. '... but it seems the final honours are saved for you.'

Chapter 6

Umar's Personality

Umar's Personality

Umar al-Faruq was an ideal Caliph. He was a just and faithful soldier in Allah's cause. He was God-fearing, trustworthy, and a secure fortress for the Islamic nation and its creed. He spent his entire period of Caliphate in the service of Islam. At the same time, he was the commander-in-chief of the army, a proficient jurist whose opinions were referred to by everyone. He was a fair and impartial judge, a merciful and compassionate father figure for all his subjects.

He was an experienced and polished statesman. He was a wise and resolute administrator. He fortified the nation with his leadership which led to the great victories against the Persians and the Romans. He conquered the entire Syria and Egypt from the Romans. Islam entered in most of the lands surrounding the Arabian Peninsula. His caliphate was an unbreakable barrier against disorder and trouble whose closed gate was Umar himself. People trying to create trouble could not get to the Muslims during his lifetime nor could they raise their heads during his rule.

Umar's Supplication on his Last Pilgrimage [*Hajj*] in 23 AH

In the year 23 AH, Umar left his residence in Madinah to perform the annual pilgrimage. When Umar departed from Mina, he stopped at a place called al-Abtah. He made a heap of sand and pebbles and covered it with a part of his robe. Then he sat down on it, raised his hands towards the sky, and said, 'O Allah! I have grown old. My strength has waned. The people under my care have become scattered. Take me [in death] before I commit any act of neglect or heedlessness.' Then he returned to Madinah.

Umar's Desire for Martyrdom

Umar ibn al-Khattab supplicated, 'O Allah! Grant me martyrdom in Your way and let my death occur in the city of Your Prophet.' It is important to realize that wishing for martyrdom is entirely different than wishing for death. The difference is that wishing for death is a request for death to be brought earlier than its appointed time. A long life is always good for a person. Wishing for martyrdom is to ask for the death of a martyr at the end of one's lifetime. It does not include the wish for death to occur before its appointed time. It is rather to desire a virtuous death.

The Last Friday Sermon Delivered by Umar

Umar delivered the Friday sermon on 21, Dhul Hijjah, 23 AH. It was the last sermon of his life. Umar told the Muslims of a dream he had seen and he himself interpreted it for them. He said to them during the sermon, 'I have seen a dream. I think it signals my death. I saw myself being pecked by a rooster twice, and that some people asked me to appoint a successor who would be the Caliph after me. Allah, the Most High will not let His religion, Caliphate, and what He sent His Prophet with, be destroyed. If I die, then the Caliph should be selected with the consultation of the six men with whom the Prophet ﷺ was well pleased when he died.

Umar's Prohibition of Letting Captives of War Stay in Madinah

Umar did not allow captives of war from conquered lands to enter the capital. Hence, the Zoroastrians of Iraq and Persia and the Christians of Syria [the Levant] and Egypt were forbidden from staying in Madinah, unless

they become Muslims and entered the Faith. This policy shows his wisdom and foresight, since these were a defeated and overthrown people. They were filled with revenge for Islam and hated it. They were prepared to conspire and plot against Islam and Muslims.

Umar stopped them from residing in the capital to secure Muslims from their evil. Some Companions of the Prophet ﷺ, however, had taken some of these non-Muslim captives as personal slaves. Some of them used to plead with Umar to allow them to keep some of these slaves in Madinah to help them in their work. So Umar let some of them stay in Madinah, although he did not like the idea. And what Umar had expected and warned against took place.

The Murder
of Umar ibn al-Khattab

The cause of Umar's murder was as follows: Al-Mughirah ibn Shu'bah, who was the governor of Kufah, had a Persian slave named Feroz Abu Lu'lu'ah. He was a native of Nihawand. He was a highly skilled worker. He was a carpenter, smith, and sculptor. Al-Mughirah wished to let him work in Madinah and to profit from his earnings. Under Islamic law, the owner of a slave was entitled to a certain share in the latter's gains.

Although Umar had previously forbidden adult non-Muslim foreigners to reside in the capital of the Islamic Empire, he consented to al-Mughirah's request. He hoped that the people of Madinah would benefit by the Persian slave's skills. Abu Lu'lu'ah set up his trade and prospered. He used to make mills. He was a Magian [Zoroastrian]. Al-Mughirah used to take four *Dirhams* from his daily earnings, which was quite reasonable.

One day, the slave complained to the Caliph that his master charged him too high a tax. Umar found out that the Persian's earnings were far above the sum demanded by al-Mughirah, from him. Umar held that the tax was not excessive. Nevertheless, Umar intended to plead with al-Mughirah on behalf of the slave. For the present, however, he advised the slave to behave well. This seeming indifference roused the slave's anger, and when Umar asked whether he would build him a windmill, the slave answered darkly: 'I will make you such a mill people will talk of it in the whole world.' Umar understood that this was a threat, but he did not pay any attention to it.

double-bladed dagger

Abu Lu'lu'ah provided himself with a double-bladed dagger and hid it in the mosque. On the morning of Wednesday, 27 Dhul Hijjah, 23 AH [5 November,

644 CE], he stabbed Umar during the dawn prayer.

Amr bin Maymûn says, 'On the morning when he [Umar ibn al-Khattab] was killed, I was standing in the mosque ready for prayer. Between him and me there was but Abdullah ibn Abbas. While passing between the rows, Umar said, 'Adjust your ranks!' then when he saw that there was no empty space in them, he advanced and recited the *Takbir*. He usually recited *Sûrah Yusuf* or *an-Nahl* [The Bee] during the first *Rak'ah* so that the people might have time to assemble. However, this time, he had only pronounced the *Takbir*, when I heard him cry out, on being stabbed, 'The dog has killed me! (– or, bitten me).'

Thereupon, the foreign infidel fled with the double-bladed dagger in his hand and did not pass anyone on his right or left without stabbing him, until he stabbed thirteen men, seven of whom died. On seeing this, a man from the Muslims threw his hooded cloak [*Bûrnûs*] over him; and when the infidel knew that he was caught, he killed himself.

Now, Umar took the hand of Abdur Rahman ibn Awf and made him advance as Imâm. Whoever was near Umar saw what I had seen but the people in the remote parts of the mosque saw nothing, except that they missed Umar's voice. They were saying: 'Glory be to Allah! Glory be to

Allah! [*Sub'han-Allah, Sub'han-Allah*]

This speaks a great deal about the discipline of those early Muslims that the turmoil caused in the front ranks by the murder of Umar and several other men did not break up the congregation, only those who were in the front ranks left their places. The rows further down the mosque remained standing as they were. It is important to realize that the expression *Sub'han-Allah* 'Glory be to Allah', is used when members of the congregation think that the *Imâm* has committed an error in his recitation or in the ritual of prayer. Held by the sense of discipline, the Muslims present in the mosque did not come to know what had happened in front. They probably thought that their *Imâm* had forgotten the words of the Qur'anic text he was reciting and stopped too long to remember them.

Then Abdur Rahman ibn Awf led the prayer and he shortened it. When the congregation had dispersed, Umar said, 'O Ibn Abbas! See who it was who killed me. So Ibn Abbas went round, and then he came back and said, "The slave of al-Mughirah.' Umar exclaimed, 'That skilled craftsman?' Ibn Abbas answered, 'Yes!' Umar remarked, 'May Allah curse him! Praise be to Allah! He has not caused me to die at the hand of a man who claimed to be a Muslim. O Ibn Abbas! It was you and your father who desired that there should be many foreign infidels in

Madinah.'

Thereafter, Umar was taken home. Before this day, the people had never suffered such a calamity. One said, 'It is nothing serious.' And another said, 'I fear for him.' It is recorded that Umar subsequently fainted, and his companions thought that he was going to die that very moment. Then one of them suggested that they should recite the call to Prayer, for this was something that Umar loved most, and it would revive him. They did so and. Umar regained consciousness, looked around, and said, 'The Prayer? O Allah! There is no place for him in Islam who gives up Prayer.' And although he was bleeding profusely, he performed his ablution and offered the prayer of dawn, which he had missed.

> "Praise be to Allah! He has not caused me to die at the hand of a man who claimed to be a Muslim"

Some beverage of dates was brought to him. He drank it but it came out from his belly. Obviously, his stomach was cut. Then milk was brought to him. He drank it and it also came out through his wound. Thus, they knew that he would die.

People poured in, praising him. A young man came and said, 'O Commander of the Faithful! Rejoice at the announcement, which Allah gave you on account of your companionship with the Messenger of Allah and your rank in Islam. Then you became caliph, and you were just. Now it is your martyrdom.'

Umar was one of the ten Companions to whom the Prophet ﷺ had announced in their lifetime that they would gain Paradise. Then Umar said to his son, 'O Abdullah ibn Umar! Find out how much debt there is upon me.' They counted it and fixed that it was eighty-six thousand [*Dirhams:* silver coins] or so.

Abdur Rahman ibn Awf is reported to have asked Umar the purpose for which he had spent that amount. This was because Umar's own lifestyle was extremely frugal. Umar explained that he had spent it on several pilgrimages - he had performed them with a large following of poor people -- and for some emergencies of State. It is clear that it was not a personal expenditure. Umar could have well regarded it as spent in the interest of the community of which he was the head. However, his uncommonly keen sense of responsibility demanded of him that the above expenditure, which did not come under any of the usual budgetary headings, should be paid from his own means.

Then Umar said, 'If the property of Umar's family be enough, repay it from their possessions. If it is not enough, demand it from Banu Adi ibn Ka'b [Umar's clan]. If their possessions are not enough, demand it from the Quraysh. But do not appeal to others beside them.'

It is important to realize that according to the ancient Arab code of honour, the clan and the tribe of a deceased debtor were normally responsible for the payment of his debt. Umar ibn al-Khattab continued, 'Thus you should repay this debt on my behalf. And go to Ai'shah, Mother of the Believers, and say: 'Umar offers you his greeting, and do not say "the Commander of the Faithful", for today I am no Commander of the Faithful. And say: Umar ibn al-Khattab asks permission to be buried beside his two Companions. Thereupon, Abdullah ibn Umar went to Ai'shah. He greeted her and asked leave to enter. He then went in and found her sitting and weeping. Abdullah said, 'Umar ibn al-Khattab offers you his greeting and asks his permission to be buried beside his two Companions.' This meant the Prophet ﷺ and Abu Bakr, whose graves were within Ai'shah's apartment. She said, 'I had desired it for myself, but today I shall give him preference over myself.'

Abdullah returned and told Umar, 'O Commander of the Faithful, she has given permission.' Umar replied,

'Praise be to Allah! There was nothing which caused me more anxiety than this! Hence, when my end comes, bear me to Ai'shah's place, then give your greetings and say: "Umar ibn al-Khattab asks permission to enter." If she gives permission, bear me inside, and if she refuses me, bring me back to the graveyard of the Muslims.'

Then the men who were around him said, 'O Commander of the Faithful, make your will. Appoint your successor.' Thereupon, Umar said, 'I do not see anyone worthier of this office than these persons or people with whom the Messenger of Allah remained pleased unto his death. And he named Ali, Uthmân, az-Zubayr, Talhah, Sa'd, and Abdur Rahman.'

These six belonged to the ten Companions who were given the glad tidings of Paradise in their lifetime. The other four were Umar himself, Abu Bakr, Abu Ubaydah ibn al-Jarrah and Sa'id ibn Zayd. When Umar expired, they bore him away to Ai'shah. Abdullah ibn Umar greeted her and said, 'Umar ibn al-Khattab asks permission to enter.' She said, 'Bring him in.' Then, he was brought in and laid there to rest beside his two Companions.

Activity

Answer the following questions:

1. Mention a few character traits of Umar رضي الله عنه.
2. How is wishing for martyrdom different from wishing for death?
3. What was Umar's wisdom in keeping the war captives away from Madinah?
4. Why did the congregation stay in its place?
5. What made the Companions believe that Umar would not live?

Write 'True' or 'False':

1. Umar predicted his death during his Last Sermon. __________
2. Umar was stabbed during the *Dhuhr* Prayer. ______________
3. Umar's assassin was never caught. ______________
4. Umar's debt was due to personal expenditure. ______________
5. Umar was buried beside the Prophet ﷺ. ____________ ______________

Fill in the blanks:

1. After stabbing Umar, Abu Lu'lu'ah stabbed ________________ men.
2. After fainting, Umar was brought to by calling out the _______________________.
3. The graves of the Prophet ﷺ, Abu Bakr, and later Umar, are in the apartment of _________________.

Chapter 7

A New Method to Select

The Caliph

A New Method to Select The Caliph

Umar continued to work for the unity of the nation and its future even until his last moments, in spite of the pain he suffered from his deep wounds. These moments shed light on his profound Faith, sincerity, and self-sacrifice. In these painful moments, he devised a new, unprecedented way to elect the new Caliph. It was a soul-stirring proof and clear sign of his leadership.

Allah's Messenger ﷺ left the people in a state when Abu Bakr was unanimously accepted to be the most meritorious of his Companions. Hence, there was little chance of disagreement on the issue of his leadership. This was because the Prophet ﷺ himself had indicated by words and actions that Abu Bakr was the most suitable leader. When Abu Bakr decided to appoint his successor, he knew that all the Companions were certain that the strongest, ablest, and best person for such a responsible position would be Umar. He consulted the prominent Companions and none of them opposed his suggestion. Everyone pledged allegiance to Umar.

Rashidun Caliphate (dark green) at its peak in 654, including its vassal states (light green)

In turn, when Umar was asked to appoint the successor on his deathbed, he thought about it deeply. He decided to follow a method, which was most suitable in the circumstances.

He appointed a council of six Companions.

The Electoral [Connected with Elections] Council: [*Ash-Shûra*]

Umar appointed a six-man advisory council called the *Shûra,* consisting of the following members:

1. Ali ibn Abi Talib
2. Uthmân bin Affan
3. Abdur Rahman bin Awf
4. Sa'd bin Abi Waqqas
5. Az-Zubayr bin al-Awwam
6. Talhah bin Ubaydullah

These six men were prominent Companions of the Prophet ﷺ. They had participated in the first battle of

Islam, the Battle of Badr. Allah's Messenger ﷺ was pleased with them when he died. All of them were fit to be leaders of the Muslim nation and were all suitable candidates for the office of the Caliph.

Umar, as we have pointed out earlier, introduced a new method for electing the Caliph. He set the time limit for it and also appointed an arbiter to watch over the process, and how to reach a decision if the votes fell equal to multiple candidates. He appointed a detachment of soldiers to monitor the electoral process in the council. He empowered the soldiers to punish anyone who opposed the decision of the council, and to prevent disorder by preventing anyone from entering or listening to the workings of the council.

Method of Electing the Caliph

Umar commanded the six-man advisory council [*ash-Shûra*] to meet in the house of one of them and start deliberations. He also sent his son Abdullah to be present there as an advisor only, without being a decision-maker or candidate. Umar did not make Sa'id bin Zayd bin Nufayl a member of the council even though he was one of the ten Companions who were promised Paradise by the Prophet. This was perhaps because Sa'id belonged to Umar's tribe, Banu Adi.

For Umar, the question of the Caliphate was a matter of religious duty alone, and he never let any of his relatives benefit by his position. Umar appointed Suhayb ar-Rûmi to lead the people in Prayers during the period of the council's session. He appointed al-Miqdad bin al-Aswad and Abu Talhah al-Ansari as observers to the election process.

Duration of Election: Deliberations

Umar specified three days as enough time for the council to come to its decision. If they took longer, it would mean that the differences would grow. Hence, he commanded them, 'Let not the fourth day come, except that you should have a leader.' Umar recommended his son Abdullah to be present at the council such that he would have no decision-making role. However, he told them, 'If three of them agree on one of them to be the leader while the remaining three agree on a different man, then let Abdullah bin Umar be the decider. Whichever of the two parties Abdullah bin Umar decides in favour of, let their choice be accepted by all.' Umar then added, 'If they are not satisfied with Abdullah's decision, then let the opinion of that group prevail which contains Abdur Rahman bin Awf.' He went on to describe Abdur Rahman as wise and rightly guided. Thus, Umar established a new workable process based on consultation. It was an excellent and most proper method according to the circumstances.

Uthmân bin Affan Elected as Successor

Abdur Rahman bin Awf and other members of the council consulted most of the people of Madinah and those Muslims who had come to Madinah for pilgrimage. They also kept in mind the opinions of governors and the people of places distant from Madinah, while making the decision. It was generally found that most of the people favoured either Uthmân or Ali to succeed Umar. However, Abdur Rahman finally decided that Uthmân bin Affan should succeed because of his age and experience. Uthmân was more than twenty-five years older than Ali. Abdur Rahman declared his allegiance in favour of Uthmân, and this was followed by Ali. Nobody opposed this decision. Thus, Uthmân became the third caliph.

Date of Death and Umar's Age at that Time

Umar was martyred on Wednesday, with three or four days remaining of Dhul Hijjah [the last month of Islamic Calendar] 23 AH. At that time his age was sixty-three years. His Caliphate lasted for thirteen and a half years and a few days.

The Prophet of Allah ﷺ died when he was 63 years old. Abu Bakr died when he was 63 years old and similarly, Umar was killed when he was 63 years old.

Suhayb bin Sinan led the Funeral Prayer for Umar. Suhayb had been leading people in obligatory Prayers, so the people asked him to lead Umar's Funeral Prayer. It is significant to note that Umar did not ask any of the six council members eligible for the caliphate to lead the Prayers. This was because it would have made the people think that he was the one chosen by Umar to be the caliph. Moreover, Suhayb had a high standing in the eyes of Umar and the other Companions.

Character of Umar and Achievements of his Caliphate

Umar's life sketch requires a few lines. Simplicity and duty were his guiding principles. Impartiality and faithfulness were the leading features of his administration. Responsibility so weighed upon him that he was heard to exclaim, 'O that my mother had not borne me; would that I had been this stalk of grass instead!'

His sense of justice was strong. No act of cruelty or injustice is recorded against him. His choice of commanders and governors was free from unfairness. His strong arm maintained the discipline of law. Conflicts were kept in check, and never dared disturb Islam until he had passed away. He kept the most prominent Companions by him in Madinah. This was, no doubt, partly to strengthen his counsels, and partly from an unwillingness to lower their dignity by placing them in office subordinate to himself.

Whip in hand, he would walk about the streets and markets of Madinah ready to punish offenders on the spot. However, with all this, he was tenderhearted. Countless acts of kindness are recorded about him, such as relieving the needs of the widows and orphans.

Once, journeying in the country during a famine, he came upon a poor woman and her hungry weeping children seated round a fire, upon which was an empty pot. Umar hastened onto the next village, obtained bread and meat, filled the pot, and cooked an ample meal, leaving the little ones laughing and at play.

Umar did not wrong, oppress, or physically hurt any person. He kept account of the smallest and most seemingly insignificant of deeds. If he even imagined that he had wronged somebody, he would seek out that person and order him to exact his revenge. Umar used to say, 'Were a goat to die on the shore of the River Euphrates, I would become afraid that Allah would hold Umar accountable for that death.'

Umar was the first o assume the title of *'Amir al-Mu'minin'* or 'Commander of the Faithful'.

Achievements of Umar's Caliphate

Umar was a wise, yet grand visionary who introduced many new ideas and changes. His reign in particular is held as a classic example by later generations for a number of significant reasons.

Primary among these reasons is the common

consensus among the majority of Muslims that Umar best exemplified and carried into effect the moral, social, and political purposes envisioned by the Glorious Qur'an. The evaluation of Umar and his far-sighted policies is captured in a statement attributed to the Messenger of Allah, 'If Allah had wished that there be a prophet after me, it would have been Umar.' The Prophet ﷺ is also reported to have said to Umar, 'O Ibn al-Khattab! By Him in whose Hand is my soul! If Satan were to encounter you on some path, he would certainly take a way different from yours.' The Prophet ﷺ also said, 'Allah has placed the truth on the tongue of Umar and into his heart.'

Effect of his Death on the Muslims

Umar's death was a terrible disaster for the Muslims. What made his assassination even more terrible was that it took place in the mosque, while he was leading the Morning Prayer. Amr bin Maimun said, 'It was as if people had never been afflicted with a calamity before that day.'

Ibn Abbas said that he did not pass by any group of people, except, that he found them weeping, as if they had lost their firstborn children.

Abdullah bin Mas'ud said, 'Umar was the fortress of Islam. People used to enter it and not come out of it.'

Achievements of his Caliphate

Umar ibn al-Khattab rightly deserves to be placed on top in a list of rulers, conquerors, and administrators. History has reported no equal of him. Most conquerors were poor rulers and administrators. Their influence on people hardly lasted after them.

There were four significant aspects of Umar's life: his personal life, his military achievements, his administrative affairs and his religious opinions.

His Personal Life

He was born thirteen years after the Prophet ﷺ and lived thirteen years after him. He was a man of extraordinary built. He appeared like a rider when standing in a crowd. Altogether, he married seven (or eight) women at different times, of whom the most prominent was Umm Kulthum, the daughter of Ali ibn Abi Talib. He had thirteen children, of whom the best known are Hafsah and Abdullah.

As he grew up, he went into business and soon became a successful trader. He showed his intelligence early as he was chosen to judge between feuding factions in Makkah. Sometimes, he represented the Quraysh as their diplomat.

In the beginning, he was staunchly opposed to the Prophet ﷺ. Disturbed by his slave-girl embracing Islam, he beat her furiously, ending with the words, 'I am not ceasing because of mercy, but because I am tired.'

Once he saw a woman of his clan preparing to migrate to Abyssinia [Ethiopia] to seek refuge there. He asked her in a voice filled with sorrow and remorse, 'Are you leaving?' she said, 'Yes, O Umar, your people have made our lives unliveable.' This was the first time she noticed grief in his voice. Aided by grief, it was not too long before he embraced Islam. This was the seventh year of the Prophet's mission.

Another prominent personality of Makkah, Hamzah, an uncle of the Prophet ﷺ, also happened to embrace Islam around the same time. Upon Umar's insistence, the Prophet ﷺ and his men arrived at the Grand Mosque to pray openly before the pagans. They ground their teeth in anger, but there was little else they could do, what with Umar and Hamzah among them.

It is said that the Prophet ﷺ named him *al-Farûq* that day because he distinguished between Islam and disbelief.

He was the only one who emigrated to Madinah openly having announced his intention.

Umar as Caliph

Assuming his position after Abu Bakr's death, Umar said in one of his first speeches,

'O people, recite the Qur'an, you will gain knowledge. Live by it so that you become its companions. Take yourself to account before you are taken account of. Prepare yourself for the day when nobody will be able to hide himself. Let no one be of such a status in your eyes that you obey him in disobedience to Allah.'

The first action that Umar took after assuming the caliphate was to return the Arab prisoners of the *Riddah* or Apostasy Wars to their families. It was an extremely wise political step. It opened the hearts of thousands for Islam. It prepared their hearts to participate in battles against disbelief or *Kufr*. During his rule, he maintained absolute justice and treated everyone equally in law.

Umar's justice and equal treatment of everyone is unique. A Ghassani prince, a new entrant into the fold of Islam, treated honourably by Umar, went for Umrah during which a Bedouin stepped on his cloak. He struck him in the face, which made his nose bleed. The man complained to Umar who asked the Ghassani to either work out a compromise with the Bedouin or face just retribution, which consisted of the Bedouin hitting him. The Ghassani was shocked. He said it was unthinkable, because he was a prince and the other a camel herdsman. He threatened that he would rather turn Christian if it was carried out. Umar told him coldly he would be executed if he apostatized. The prince sought time, and taking shelter of the darkness of the night, escaped to Constantinople with his attendants, although later he regretted deeply for having fled.

Once he found a blind Jew begging. He gave the reason for his begging as extreme poverty and the inability to pay *Jizyah* or the Protection Tax. Umar gave him something from his own house. Then he sent him to the Treasury with instructions that he and others like him be given allowances from the Treasury and the Protection Tax burden removed from them. His words are of historic significance: 'It does not befit us that we use them in their youth, and then abandon them to begging in their old age.'

Abdullah bin Aamir reported, 'I travelled with Umar from Madinah to Makkah and then back. Nowhere on the way did he pitch a tent. He would stretch a piece of leather on the ground and using a cloak to cover would sleep under a tree.

Umar and his Establishment of the *Diwan* or the State Treasury

One of the major innovations undertaken by Umar during his rule as Caliph was the establishment of the state register of pensions known as *Diwan*. Its purpose was to distribute the increasing revenues pouring into the state treasury effectively and equitably.

Among other civic and legal acts, Umar established the Islamic Calendar [*Hijri*] dating the beginning of the Islamic era to the Prophet's emigration in 622 CE.

During the thirteen and a half years of his caliphate, Umar made a remarkable contribution in the history of Islam. Under his leadership, Islam spread to many lands. He divided the Muslim-controlled regions into eight provinces. He appointed efficient and pious governors to all those provinces. Following the example of Abu Bakr, Umar used to draw the minimum possible wage from the public treasury. He also fixed the salaries of the governors. When the income of the government increased significantly, he made arrangements to distribute the wealth to the common people. He fixed an allowance for everybody in Madinah. The Muslims who had been the foremost in accepting Islam, who had made the *Hijrah* and participated in the battles received larger allowances than those who embraced Islam later.

Along with the governors, he appointed judges for each of the provinces. During the reign of Umar, Islam had spread to Iraq, Syria, Palestine, Egypt, and many parts of Iran and Central Asia. Still, the Muslims had a large number of non-Muslim populations under their rule. There were general guidelines in the Qur'an and the *Sunnah* of the Prophet ﷺ about the status of non-Muslims. There was, however, a need to define relations with non-Muslims and decide their status in Muslim society. Umar developed several specific laws regarding non-Muslims, which were followed by later generations.

Relations with the People of the Book

Ahl al-Kitâb is an Arabic term that means 'People of the Book' or 'Scriptures'. They are the Jews and Christians, also known in Arabic as *Ahl adh-Dhimmah*: the Protected People [sing. *Dhimmi*].

You would recall that the Christians of Jerusalem insisted that they would surrender to the Caliph Umar in person. Umar travelled to Jerusalem for this purpose and assured the freedom of religion to non-Muslims there. He also made sure that the churches and places of worship were not destroyed by Muslims or converted into mosques. This was made very clear in the agreement drawn up by the Caliph upon the surrender of Jerusalem in 638 CE, the terms of which read:

> 'In the Name of Allah, the Merciful, the Compassionate.
>
> This is the security which Umar, the servant of Allah, the Commander of the Faithful, grants to the people of *Ilya* [*Ilya* is the ancient name for Jerusalem]. He grants to all, whether sick or sound, security for their lives, their possessions, their churches and their crosses, and for all that concerns their religion. Their churches shall not be changed into dwelling places, nor destroyed, neither shall they nor their parts be in anyway diminished, nor the crosses of the inhabitants nor anything of their possessions, nor shall any restriction be placed upon them in the matter of their Faith, nor shall anyone of them be harmed.'

It is further recorded that Umar visited the holy places in Jerusalem in the company of the Patriarch of the city. When the time for Prayer came, the Patriarch kindly invited the caliph to offer his Prayer in the Church of

Resurrection. Umar declined saying that if we were to do that later, Muslims might wrongfully claim the church as their own place of worship. This shows how tolerant and considerate Umar was!

The Muslims needed to run the government, and for that they required funds. This was collected in the form of taxes from the citizens. Muslims used to pay the *Zakât* for this purpose. It was also their duty to fight for the state when the need arose. Non-Muslims were not required to do either of the two. The Muslims instituted a tax called *Jizyah* or Protection Tax for non-Muslims. Adult able-bodied males from the People of the Book were required to pay the head-tax or *Jizyah* in return for state protection of their rights. Women, minors, the infirm, old, destitute, and religious personages, like monks, were normally exempted from its payment. State Funds were often distributed for the maintenance of poor Jews and Christians. Their maintenance was consequently a basic, humane responsibility of the Muslim rulers. Muslims were both morally responsible for the safety of non-Muslims.

It is recorded that Umar recognized two categories of poor and desperate people who qualified for state support: the *Fuqara* [the poor] who were Muslims, and the *Masâkin* [the destitute] who were the People of the Book residing in Islamic realms.

In this connection, a very touching anecdote is related about Umar, which we have mentioned briefly earlier. Umar once encountered an old, blind Jewish man begging for alms and brought him to his home out of pity. He gave the destitute man a modest sum of money from his own funds as alms. Upon inquiry, Umar learnt that the Jew had been paying taxes to the state. Shocked, Umar declared this to be injustice. He then ordered the state treasury to immediately stop and to treat him instead as one of the penniless People of the Book entitled to state maintenance.

Umar's practice allowed later jurists to conclude that non-Muslims, like Muslims, had certain claims on the Islamic state for their basic welfare and sustenance. Thus, Umar was merciful and tolerant in his treatment of the People of the Book and he set a valuable example for the succeeding generations.

Women's Treatment

During his Caliphate, Umar appointed a woman, Shifa bint Abdullah, as the inspector of markets in Madinah, a position roughly equivalent to that of a city mayor. Umar also humbly and publicly accepted an elderly woman's legal opinion as valid over his own. According to this account, Umar once tried to impose a ceiling on the value of the dower on *Mahr* to be given to the bride by the groom, which was met with vigorous opposition. When Umar made an announcement to this effect in the mosque at Madinah, an older woman rebuked him and accused him of taking back what Allah and His Messenger had given them. The humbled Caliph admitted his mistake in public by saying, 'Umar is wrong and this woman is right.' This anecdote shows that he was not above taking criticism from women when it was well-deserved and right.

Umar was known for his strong personality. One day, a man quarrelled with his wife and came to Umar to ask him his advice on how to deal with her. When he stood at Umar's door and was about to knock, he heard Umar's wife shouting at him, while Umar remained silent. He neither shouted back, nor rebuked her!

The man was amazed, and turned back to leave. Umar heard a noise at the door, so he came out and called the man, 'What do you need?'

He said, 'O *Amir al-Mu'minin*, I came to you to complain about my wife, but then I heard your wife shouting at you.' Umar said, 'She is my wife who attempts to perform all her wifely duties perfectly, makes me food and washes my clothes. Shall I not be patient with her?'

It was Umar, after all, who had entrusted the Qur'an

manuscript in his possession, which formed the basis for the final version of the Qur'anic text to the safekeeping of his daughter, Hafsah, rather than to that of one of his sons.

Umar was an exemplary ruler. He belonged to the circle of the foremost true friends of the Prophet ﷺ. He was one of the most outstanding statesmen not only in the history of Islam, but in world history. He was a man of the utmost willpower, keenest sense of duty, tireless energy, and an organizer of the first rank.

The Muslim *Ummah* as well as the non-Muslims lived very happily and peacefully under the leadership of Umar. During his rule, Islam spread and prospered.

Activity

Answer the following questions:

1. What do you know about '*ash-Shura*'? Who were its members?
2. Why did Umar not make Sa'id bin Zaid bin Nufayl a member of the Council?
3. How was Uthmān elected as the Caliph by the Council?
4. What was Umar's wisdom in not choosing a Coun cil member as Imām?
5. What is the *Diwan*? What was its purpose?
6. What do you mean by Scriptuaries? How did Umar deal with them?
7. Mention a few points about how Umar treated women.

Fill in the blanks

1. Umar specified ______________ days as enough time for the Council to reach a decision.
2. Umar established the *Hijri* or the Islam________________, based on the Prophet's ________________ to Madinah.
3. Ilyaistheancientnamefor__________________.
4. Funds to run the government were taken from the Muslims through the payment of ___________________ and from the non-Muslims through ____________________.

5. Umar recognized two categories of poor and desperate people: the ________________ who were the Muslims, and the ________________________who were the People of the Book.

Refer to Context

1. 'O that my mother had not borne me…'
2. 'It was as if people had never been afflicted with a calamity before that day.'

Do-It-Yourself

- Read up the brief incidences and anecdotes from the lesson and flesh out a character sketch of Umar. What qualities of this great role model would you strive to imbibe?

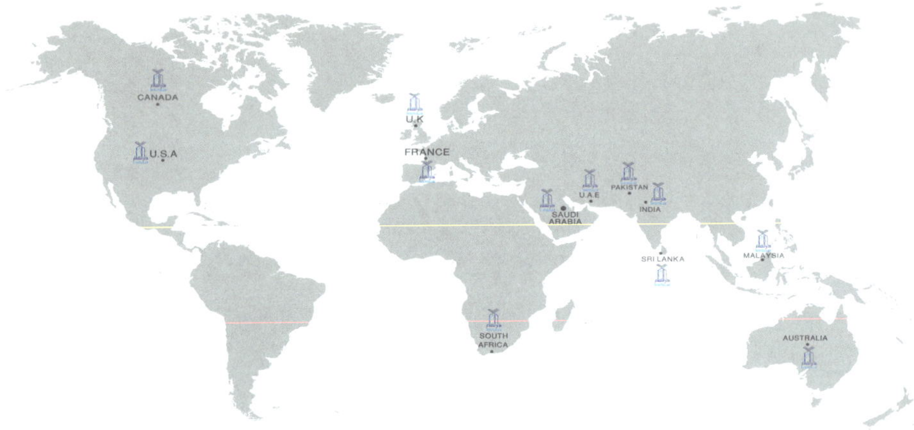

DARUSSALAM

GLOBAL LEADER IN ISLAMIC PUBLICATION